the Blue Shoal Inn

CORAL ISLAND
BOOK THREE

LILLY MIRREN

Epub ISBN: 978-1-922650-17-7

Paperback ISBN: 978-1-922650-19-1

Version 1.0

Published by Black Lab Press 2022

Lilly Mirren has asserted her right to be identified as the author of this Work in accordance with the Copyright, Designs and Patents Act 1988.

This is a work of fiction. Names, characters, organisations, places, events and incidents are either products of the author's imagination or are used fictitiously. Any resemblance to actual persons, living or dead, or actual events is purely coincidental.

Cover design by Erin D'Ameron Hill.

First published worldwide by Black Lab Press in 2022.

Brisbane, Australia.

www.blacklabpress.com

About The Blue Shoal Inn

The *Blue Shoal Inn* faces its biggest challenge yet. Will it close its doors, or will Taya find a way to save it?

Taya's inn is under threat. Her father's company has built a five star resort in Blue Shoal and is taking her business. She renovates the inn, as a last ditch effort to keep it afloat, but will finally have to make a decision about whether to hold onto the past or embrace the future.

When her father hires a handsome manager for his new resort, Taya wants to hate him but witnesses him do something unexpected that causes everything she thought she believed to unravel.

Rowan reconnects with his estranged stepfather, Buck, but questions still hang over Buck's head about the murder of Penny's grandmother. He was once a suspect, but was cleared of any wrongdoing. Still, Penny and her friends do some digging and will discover that not everything is as it seems. When, Rowan and Penny have a decision to make that could mean big changes for both of them, they'll learn a truth about their past that has been hidden for far too long.

Please note: this book is written using Australian English. Some words, spelling and phrases may be unfamiliar to you.

One

THERE WAS a slight breeze along the beach when Taya Eldridge stepped outside the *Blue Shoal Inn*'s back door and onto the large deck that edged the wide, sparkling blue infinity pool. She'd had the pool installed five years earlier to try to keep pace with the developments in Blue Shoal before they put her quaint seaside destination out of business. And for a while, she'd succeeded. Keeping the building updated but retaining the rustic, retro appeal of the place had made it a must-visit destination for returning families and romance-inspired couples. But times were changing.

There were no guests in the swimming pool area, since it was the end of autumn and the weather had turned cooler. The afternoon sun set the ocean ablaze as Taya slipped out of her towel and into the pool. The water was cold, but the sun still warm enough that it was pleasant to be out of doors and spending some time relaxing. She hadn't relaxed much over the past twenty years. Caring for her sick husband, then managing their affairs and running the business after his death, had occupied all her time. But lately the inn had been quieter, with fewer guests every week. She'd had more time to herself. More time to think.

Mostly what she thought about was how to save her business and whether it was what she wanted. She'd never have believed that would be a question. It'd been her and Todd's dream to renovate the old place when they'd bought it two decades earlier. But now that she was in her mid-forties, she was tired. It was such a struggle to keep the inn afloat. There was always something broken or needing an update, some customer complaint to follow up on. And she'd lost the zest she had for it all.

She dipped beneath the surface of the water and swam a few laps up and down the length of the pool. Her body glided through the water, her arms curving in arcs. She spun with a somersault at either end, letting the water cascade over her, the tiredness seep from her muscles and the kinks from her neck. She spent far too much time these days perched in front of her computer doing accounts and running through ledgers. What she missed was having a chance to interact with people, to get out and about and enjoy her life. She'd become something of a hermit since her husband's death, and if it wasn't for her girl-friends, Beatrice, Eveleigh and Penny, she'd likely never do anything fun now that her daughter Camden had left home.

Out of breath, she paused her swim to stare at the ocean. Balancing her arms along the edge of the infinity pool, she watched tourists walking the length of the beach. A few children swam near the ocean's edge, splashing and playing. Some built sandcastles. There was a retired couple lying on towels on the sand. She seemed to recall them being in the same place hours earlier and wondered if they'd fallen asleep there. No doubt they'd be very red tomorrow.

At the other end of the beach was the resort her father had built. It was finally operational. They'd been constructing the modern white condos that stepped down the tree-covered hill for over a year, but now it was truly a thing of beauty. Taya couldn't help admiring it even as irritation flashed through her chest. She shook her head slowly as she took in the glimpse of blue pools, the perfectly shaped palm trees, the tasteful tile roofs tilting against the hillside to help the resort fade into the bush landscape around them. She hadn't walked through the completed resort yet— was still too angry that he'd chosen to build his latest resort only two hundred metres from her business. He knew how much the Blue Shoal Inn meant to her.

When she'd pointed out this oversight, he'd smiled and embraced her. "What's the matter, sweetheart? Afraid of a little competition? I'm not worried—I know you have it in you. You're an Eldridge, after all!"

His words had aggravated her beyond anything else he could've said because he was right — if the inn was such a good business, as she'd asserted when she reprimanded him, it should be able to stand on its own two feet, even with more competition in Blue Shoal. The tiny town couldn't stay small forever. Gradually people were discovering it, and the more they did, the better she should profit from her tourist business, surely. That'd been her experience over the past two decades as she built a solid returning guest list — people who came back every year or two, who said it was their favourite place to holiday. She had guests who'd raised their families spending every summer at the inn and now returned regularly as grandparents. It was what she loved most about her business — she, the staff and her guests were like one big happy family.

When Dad built his insanely romantic, luxuriously appointed and extremely tempting "Paradise Resort at Blue Shoal," their happy haven began losing guests. There were *Paradise Resorts* dotted all up and down the Queensland coast and around the world. Why did he have to build one here?

His argument had been that he'd always intended to build in the hamlet, since he lived here and was sick of travelling all the time. Also, he wanted the world to experience the Blue Shoal he loved. She often pointed out that the world was already enjoying the town when they stayed at her inn, but he only agreed with her. So instead of labouring the point, she'd said goodbye and taken a long run around the headland to calm her nerves.

Even as she studied the outline of the new resort, burnt pink by the setting sun, a man stepped out through a white gate and descended the staircase from the resort to the beach. He wore long black pants and a blue shirt tucked in at the waist. His shoes were in one hand and he tented the other hand over his eyes to cut the glare.

She watched him traverse the beach, unable to take her eyes off him. There was something very striking about his tall frame, black hair and business attire — he stood out from the crowd of swimsuit-wearing tourists. Who was he? She'd never seen him before. There weren't many men who looked or dressed like that on the island, and certainly none in Blue Shoal. The local men were generally surfers or fishermen and preferred board shorts and T-shirts.

He strode in her direction, then stopped beneath her vantage point and stared up at the building behind her. She pretended to be looking out at the ocean, but snuck a glance at him every now and then. It was disconcerting the way he studied her hotel, as though he knew everything about it. Perhaps he did. When she looked at him again, she found he was gazing at her with a broad smile lighting up his handsome face.

"Enjoying the sunset?"

Her face flushed with warmth. "Yes, very much."

"That inn is really something special," he said, letting his gaze flicker back over the structure again. He had a soft accent and pronounced his words precisely.

She spun halfway around to look at it herself. The paint

4

needed to be redone. The roof was clearly in need of repair, and there were parts that sagged. But the bones of the building were excellent, at least according to the inspector she'd hired to check it over every year. And she loved the intricate moulding around the windows, the steep lines of the roof. There was a character and strength to the place that she found very appealing and always had.

"They don't make them like that anymore," he continued. "I'd love to buy it."

"Really?" Her heart sank. Perhaps he was an investor with an eye on her property. She had no intention of selling it. A developer would be just as likely to tear it down and rebuild a modern monstrosity in its place as they were to remodel it.

"Mmmm..." He rubbed a hand over his chin. "But I bet the owner wouldn't sell. Apparently, she's quite a dragon."

Her eyes narrowed. "Really?"

"So they tell me."

"And who are you?" She did her best to hide her irritation with a friendly expression.

His eyes met hers. Deep brown that seemed to reach down into her soul and read her very thoughts. "I'm Andrew Reddy. I manage the Paradise Resort. Are you a guest here? Perhaps next time, you should try the Paradise. You might enjoy our twenty-four-hour spa service."

She wanted to snap that she had no need of his spa service since she had her own, but the two hours per day that she brought someone in to offer massages and facials didn't seem quite so appealing in light of what his resort could offer. She raised her chin. "Perhaps."

"Lovely to meet you," he said. Then marched back up the beach to the resort where he'd come from.

Her nostrils flared. So, Dad had hired a new manager to take over the running of his resort. That had always been his intention—she knew that. He wanted to retire, to have other people managing the various aspects of the business that he'd previously kept tightly under his control. He'd asked her to head up the resort — she'd been his first choice—but she hadn't been willing to give up on her inn. Partly because he'd scoffed at the purchase she and Todd had made so soon after they were married, telling her that she had a duty to take over the management of the family business. He'd changed his tune since then and had been nothing but supportive in recent years. And when she turned down his offer, he'd been polite and hadn't seemed bothered by it.

Now, it seemed Andrew Reddy would manage the Paradise Resort. He was to be her competitor, and he had his eye on her hotel as a possible acquisition. But there was no way she'd sell the Blue Shoal Inn to a slick city operator. He wouldn't understand her guests or the business and its history. No doubt he'd tile the floors and put hot tubs in every room. He wouldn't respect the integrity and character of the building. And she hadn't built her business for twenty years only to let someone like him tear it down overnight.

Two

"BUCK CLEMENTS BUILT MY BEACH COTTAGE?" Beatrice Rushton gaped at Betsy.

She couldn't grasp for a moment the full implications. Buck had built the cottage? The same cottage where she'd found the stash of fifty-year-old unprocessed photographs? The same Buck who was Rowan Clements's stepfather and a suspect in the murder of Penny's grandmother, Mary Brown, back in 1976?

"That can't be a coincidence..." she muttered, her hands steepled together in front of her mouth.

"What's that, dear?" Betsy had her attention half on Bea and half on her granddaughter, who was colouring with markers and getting red ink on the counter. "Don't do that, sweetheart. Here, I'll get you a piece of cardboard to lean on. That way, we can keep the counter nice and clean."

Bea gathered her thoughts while Betsy settled Samantha back into place at the counter with cardboard beneath her colouring book. Then she wiped down the counter, setting everything back to rights again.

"I'm sorry," she said. "We were in the middle of talking about something. What was that...?"

"Buck. He built the cottage where I found those photographs."

"Oh, yes. The photographs," Betsy replied. "How are you going with those? Did you figure out who was in them and why they were there?"

Bea shook her head. "Not exactly. We know who most of the people are, of course, since they're Penny's family—and Rowan's as well, it seems. In fact, Buck was in several pictures himself."

"Lovely — I forgot to wear my glasses when you showed them to me, so I couldn't pick anyone out. Where are my glasses now?" she asked, patting her pockets.

Bea arched an eyebrow and pointed to the top of Betsy's head. "Up there."

"Ah, yes, of course. Thank you, honey. Now, I'd better get along with putting together this flower arrangement or I'll be late and the client won't thank me for it."

Bea started for the door. "I won't keep you. It was nice to see you again, Betsy." Her thoughts were in a whirl. So many questions sprang to mind that she wasn't sure where to begin. Why did Betsy wait until now to tell her about Buck's involvement with the cottage?

She spun on her heel to study the florist, who'd returned to clipping the ends off a bunch of white lilies and arranging them in a tall glass vase. "Do you know why Mum would've hidden the photographs at the cottage? Was there anything significant about them?"

"Who knows? They seem like normal-enough photos to me — family, friends."

"But they were Penny's family and friends." Bea's nose wrinkled.

"That's true," Betsy mused. "It is a bit strange that Luella hid photographs of Penny's family and friends in the wall of a cottage she didn't own. But then, your mother was an odd duck sometimes."

"Saying it out loud that way, it's hard to wrap my head around," Bea admitted.

She left the flower shop and strode back to the café, her footsteps echoing on the hard pavement. The town was mostly empty of people, since the afternoon ferry had already left and school had long since finished for the day. Samantha had begun walking from the primary school to the florist's shop to spend the afternoons with her grandmother in recent weeks, and Bea could tell Betsy was over the moon about it. She'd developed something of a glow that had never been there before. Her cheeks were pink, her eyes sparkled, and she smiled far more readily than she had before when she'd been kept from seeing her granddaughter by a disgruntled son.

They'd had some kind of family conflict—Bea wasn't sure exactly what—that had kept them apart for years. She was glad they'd managed to resolve it enough that Betsy could help care for Sam, who'd been left on her own a lot of the time while her father worked on the mainland.

Bea closed up the café and farewelled her staff, then spent half an hour doing the books before giving up and heading home. On the way, she stopped off at her father's house up on the hill, overlooking the ocean. It was dark by the time she arrived, and the front porch light was on. He knew she often stopped by on her way home from work and left the light on for her. Something she appreciated given her fear of spiders and their tendency to lurk on the stairs and around the door.

The door wasn't locked, so she stepped inside, calling out to him as she did. She found him shucking oysters in the kitchen, a pair of glasses perched on top of his balding head. It reminded her instantly of her earlier conversation with Betsy, and she hid a grin as she reached into the fridge for an open bottle of white wine.

"Hi, Dad. How are you?"

"Good, thanks, love. Happy hour?"

She waved the bottle in the air, then searched for a glass. "It is indeed. I've had a long day."

"I found some oysters over at Point Prospect. They look nice and juicy."

"Sounds great," Bea replied.

She poured two glasses of wine and carried them out to the back deck, where her father was already setting up a plate of oysters on the half shell, hot sauce, crackers and horseradish.

"Where did you learn to eat oysters like that?" she asked as she sat.

"When I was in the Navy, we spent some time in Florida. This is how they do it there. It's delicious. You want me to make one for you?"

"Yes, please." She took the oyster on a cracker from him and ate it in one bite. It was delicious and fresh, with a hint of salt, and she closed her eyes to enjoy the flavour. "Mmmm."

He sipped his wine, studying her. "What happened today that made it so long?"

"Lots of customers. Tourists from the mainland, as well as a busload on their way across to Blue Shoal along the newly finished road. Apparently, it's smooth as can be now that they've graded it."

"I took a look a few days ago. It's very nice, although it changes the feel of the island. I suppose nothing stays the same forever. But I'd hoped Coral Island would never become a tourist hub."

"It's still not very busy compared to most places," Bea said as she looked out into the dark night. The moon rested low in the sky and glittered against the black ocean in the distance.

They chatted and ate for several more minutes before Bea

finally sighed and leaned back in her chair. "I don't know what to think about something Betsy told me today."

Dad arched an eyebrow. "Oh?"

"She said Buck built the beach cottage — my beach cottage."

"I thought you knew that."

"I'd forgotten, or maybe I didn't know. I'm not sure. But it changes everything."

"Does it?" He reached for another oyster.

"She also said Mum was the one who hid the photos there. She saw her leave. That's when she discovered the music box. Mum dropped it on her way out."

Dad arched an eyebrow. "That's news to me."

"You don't seem bothered," Bea said, before eating another oyster.

He shrugged. "What difference does it make now?"

Bea gaped. "What difference...? Why did Mum go there? Why did she hide the photos in the wall? Did it have anything to do with Buck? His name keeps coming up whenever we look into the murder case. There has to be some kind of connection there. Or maybe I'm looking for links where they don't exist."

Dad gulped a mouthful of wine. "I didn't know your mother hid those photos. I have no idea where she got them. But I do know she believed Buck was the one who killed Mary. She was obsessed with the idea — said she had proof, but she gave her proof to the police and it never went anywhere. They followed him up as a suspect at the time, but he was cleared. Still, she never got over it. For years, she stayed quiet. Then one day, when you were a teenager, she got all worked up over it again and started spreading the rumour around town."

Bea straightened in her seat. "Why did she do that?"

"She said she caught him looking at someone. I don't know why that upset her the way it did—I wasn't there. But the police were sick of her by then and threatened her to be quiet or they'd charge her with slander, since there was no proof of anything. The whole community started to turn on her, called her names, said she was nuts. She retreated into herself..." His eyes filled with tears, and his voice broke. He fell quiet and stared into the distance. "It's not something I like to talk about."

Bea's throat ached. She'd had no idea any of that had happened. How had she managed to ignore it all? She'd heard people calling her mother names, saying she was crazy, but she didn't know what it was all about. Even if she'd heard the rumours, she wouldn't have understood. Besides, she'd been so preoccupied with her own life and the embarrassment her mother caused her that she hadn't thought to dig deeper. The memory of that caused a dull pain in her gut.

"I wish I'd reacted differently. I'd do anything to be able to go back and know her better, to ask her questions, to dig deeper. Maybe we should've moved..." She shook her head in frustration. "It's so unfair."

Dad exhaled slowly. "I've had the same thoughts a thousand times. But we can't go back."

"I know." She studied the outline of the moon. It was a sliver against an inky backdrop, half asleep in a star-studded sky. Her heart thudded as a thought lobbed into her mind. "Why did Mum think Buck was the killer? You said she had proof. What was it?"

Dad cleared his throat. "It was Ruby Brown, Penny's mum. She joined the pregnancy support group your mum was in. She was only sixteen. Your mother kind of took her under her wing. They all did. But especially her and June, who were good friends."

"I'd figured that part out. Penny told me they met during a pregnancy class."

"Then, when her mother Mary died, Ruby was a mess. She

didn't know what to do or how to manage living without her. In class one night, when June wasn't there, Ruby was crying hard. Luella pulled her aside to comfort her, and Ruby told her the father of her child was a married man. Of course, Luella was horrified. She'd thought the father must've been one of the boys at the high school. So she asked Ruby who he was, and Ruby told her it was Buck, who by then was married to June."

"He was the father?" Bea's eyes widened in horror.

"Yep. Buck was a friend of Ruby's family. They spent time together at their beach house. They went on picnics together, fishing, swimming … you name it. Then Buck had a whirlwind romance with June when she was already pregnant with Rowan. They got married so quickly, it made our heads spin. Especially since no one knew anything about him at first. Here was this American, swooping in and saving the day with one of the local girls who'd gotten into trouble with an itinerant fisherman, and when Ruby told us what he'd done, we were both furious. I could've popped him one right in the mouth, but Luella convinced me not to."

"He raped Ruby?" Bea whispered, picturing her mother begging her father not to harm him.

"She said it wasn't rape, that they were in love, but she was sixteen years old, maybe younger when the affair started. He took advantage…" His eyes glimmered in the darkness. "When we found that out, we knew he must've killed Mary. Ruby didn't think he could've done it. After that, Luella told the police what Ruby said, and they interviewed everyone involved. But they never charged him with anything, and they said he had an alibi for the murder, so they dropped him as a suspect. No one was ever charged, and the case went cold."

"And what about Buck's new wife, June? What did she think of it all?"

"At first, she listened to our accusations, but she couldn't believe he was Penny's father, let alone a murderer. They were newlyweds, and he was kind to her. But she eventually left him. Although we didn't hear it from her, since she cut ties with us after Luella made the allegations against him."

"So Mum lost all her friends, the respect of the community, and no one listened to her?"

Dad sighed. "It was a difficult time for us all. And I'm ashamed to say, I didn't support her as well as I could've. I was trying my best to deal with the business, with you kids, to manage everything and keep it from falling apart. I was frustrated with her — told her to drop it. The police didn't find anything against him and Ruby never pressed charges, so they couldn't do anything there... It was so hard for your mother to move on and let it go."

Bea's head dropped into her hands. "Why didn't anyone tell me all this before now?"

"I guess we wanted to put it behind us. And in a way, we managed it. Until now, of course." He shot her a rueful smile. "I didn't expect you to drag it all back up again."

Three

TAYA STOOD OUTSIDE HER PARENTS' house smoking a cigarette. She hadn't smoked a cigarette since the day her husband died. She had given it up and had hardly been tempted in the decades since. But now anxiety ate at her gut, and her hands shook as she studied the modern curves of the palatial home her parents had built on the headland over-looking all of Blue Shoal.

She dropped the cigarette onto the brick driveway and stubbed it out with a toe, an act of rebellion from a teenager at heart. She knew how much her father would hate to see the cigarette lying there on his perfectly maintained driveway in his immaculately manicured garden. When she came here, she often felt as though she was a teen all over again and a well of rebellious anger bubbled up within, especially when she was frustrated with her parents and felt powerless to do anything to change the situation — exactly like she had when she was a kid.

But this time, she fully intended to speak her mind. She hated conflict and confrontation, so the cigarette was intended to bolster her nerves. All it'd done instead was make her fidget and exacerbate her asthma. She coughed as she walked up to the house and rang the doorbell. Two enormous Doberman Pinschers jogged around the outside of the house and wagged their tails to greet her. She patted their shiny black heads between their pointed ears and murmured words of greeting. Then the door opened, and a maid welcomed her inside.

"Good evening, Mother," she said, striding into the sitting room and heading immediately for the drinks cart. "Dad, good to see you."

Her father rose to greet her. "Taya, let me get you a drink."

"Thanks, Dad. I'll have a martini, please."

"Certainly." He kissed her cheek and stood with his hands on her shoulders, looking into her eyes. "You seem tired. And perhaps you'd like a mint." His brow furrowed as he shook his head and tutted his tongue. He pushed a small box of mints in her direction on the drinks cart, and she took one with a grimace.

"Thanks."

"Everything okay?" Mum asked, leaning back in her chair, martini aloft.

"All good. I've had a rough day. That's all."

"I'm sorry to hear it," Mum replied. "Come and sit down and tell me all about it."

"Actually, I wanted to talk to Dad about something as well." She sat and crossed her legs, then took a sip of martini.

Her father sat opposite her with a glass of Scotch. "Let's hear it, then."

She didn't want to be rude. Her intention was to raise the subject in a professional and appropriate manner. Her father was big on being appropriate. For him, the worst sin she could commit was to be emotional, hysterical or unprofessional.

"Thank you, Dad. I want to talk about your goal of owning my inn and adding it to your already enormous resort portfolio."

Dad's eyebrows arched. "Owning your...?"

"My business—that's right. I know that's your goal, so there's no need to pretend. And I wanted to be the one to tell you, to your face, that it's not for sale. You know how much I love the place, how many hours of work I've poured into it — along with my blood and my heart. You know I couldn't sell it, so what's the plan? Do you intend to squeeze me out?"

Dad frowned. "What? Why are you speaking this way? We're here for a nice family meal..."

"It seems very out of the blue, darling," Mum added, her brow furrowed.

Taya smoothed her skirt over her legs. "Dad knows what I'm referring to."

Dad's eyes narrowed. "I have no idea, sweetheart. Please give me a little bit more context, and maybe I can catch up."

"I met your new manager."

"You met Andrew? What do you think?"

"Handsome, isn't he?" Mum's eyes twinkled. She gulped a mouthful of martini.

Dad waved a hand. "Oh, give over. Who cares how he looks?"

"I'm just saying," Mum said, offering Taya a wink.

Taya rolled her eyes. "Yes, he's very handsome. But he's also a complete shark. He told me, point-blank, that he intends to buy the inn and add it to the Paradise Resort holdings."

"He did?" Dad asked. "Huh. I mean, we spoke about the possibility, but I certainly didn't give him permission to address it with you. We hadn't decided on a way forward."

"He didn't know I was me... It's a long story. Anyway, I hope you understand that it's not for sale, and you can get your shark to back off."

"Message received. Sweetheart, there's no need to get upset. You can always come to me with any problems you have. And if you need help with the business, you know you can ask me. Right?"

"I know that, Dad. And I really appreciate it. Honestly, I do. But I have to be able to do this myself. Yes, we're experiencing a dip in income at the moment due to your resort opening, but I'm sure things will level out once the novelty wears off. I have a very loyal customer base, and they love coming to the inn for their holidays. That won't change."

"Of course. You're absolutely right." The doorbell rang, and he stood to answer it as he spoke. "I'll make sure Andrew understands as well. In fact, here he is now."

Taya's heart skipped a beat. It was just like her parents not to give her warning of an additional guest at dinner. It'd always irritated her, but never more so than now.

The maid led Andrew into the sitting room. He was dressed more casually than the last time she'd seen him. He wore a pair of tight-fitting blue jeans, a white v-necked T-shirt and his hair was mussed.

His gaze swept the room. "Good evening, all." Then he saw Taya, and his grin faded. "The swimming pool lady."

Dad frowned. "Swimming pool?"

"Never mind," Taya said, stepping forwards with hand outstretched. "Taya Eldridge. Pleasure to meet you formally, Andrew."

He shook her hand, hesitation in his eyes. No doubt he was attempting to recall the details of their conversation.

"Don't worry," she assured him smoothly. "You didn't say anything incriminating. Other than advertising your intent to buy my inn, of course."

She laughed, and he joined her, his eyes crinkling at the edges. "Well, thank goodness for that."

"I seem to have missed something," Mum said, her lips puckered.

"We've already met," Taya explained.

"Oh, how wonderful," Mum replied. "I knew the two of you would hit it off. Didn't I say so, Cameron?"

A bemused smirk playing at the corners of Dad's mouth. "You did, Tina, and you're always right. Would you like a drink, Andrew?"

By the time she'd made it through dinner, Taya was fuming silently. She sipped her coffee out on the deck and listened as Andrew and her father discussed their respective golf games, her fingers tapping out a rhythm on the arm of her chair.

Her mother prattled on about the latest gossip from the local gym she attended religiously and where she had honed her body into an athletic and supple advertisement for Pilates classes.

"How is Camden?" Mum asked.

Taya's fingers stopped drumming. The one person whose very presence in the world calmed her nerves was her twenty-year-old daughter. Taya missed her tremendously, but knew Camden was healthy, happy and pursuing her dream to become a chef at one of her father's resorts in Cairns under the tutelage of a man Taya had known most of her life. Taya had named her daughter after her father, which had been a source of joy for him ever since.

"She seems happy," Taya said. "I spoke to her yesterday, and she's tired. They've been working long hours. But she's excited about what she's learning. She's made some good friends in the industry too, so they have the same crazy hours and go to the movies or take walks together in the middle of the day after the lunch rush. They even spend their days off snorkelling on the reef sometimes."

"That's good to hear," Mum replied. "It's about time she came home for a visit, though. We haven't seen her in so long."

"She doesn't have any leave accumulated."

"Don't worry—I know the boss. I'm sure I can arrange something," Mum replied, crossing her arms.

Taya rolled her eyes. "No, Mum. We agreed Cam wouldn't get any special privileges from being the owner's granddaughter. She doesn't want that. She wants the other staff to accept her as one of their own, and so far, she's gotten away with her secret since her surname is different to ours."

Her mother pouted. "I don't understand why she wouldn't want to take advantage of the Eldridge name."

Taya patted her mother's arm. "I know you don't, Mum. But we have to respect her wishes."

She glanced up and found Andrew's gaze on her. His dark brown eyes were slightly narrowed, and he wore a curious expression that disappeared the moment she locked eyes with him. The mocking look returned, and he dipped his head in acknowledgement as irritation washed over her. The man was obnoxious and annoying without even uttering a word. She had no idea what her father saw in him, but clearly he wasn't to be trusted.

Four

PENNY'S LEG rested on the beanbag in front of her couch. She resisted the overwhelming urge to scratch her toes. It would take an effort she didn't have the energy for beneath the moon boot. In the kitchen, the kettle finished boiling, and she listened to the sounds of Rowan rustling about, no doubt looking for cups and tea bags, sugar and spoons. She hated that he was waiting on her. She should be in there making the tea — after all, it was her kitchen. Also, she didn't like being an invalid. It was extremely frustrating, although she had to admit, it'd been nice that he'd been around so much more than usual.

Within minutes, Rowan was back in the living room, carrying a tray. He set it down on the coffee table and handed Penny a cup of hot tea. Steam tickled her nostrils as she sipped it tentatively. He'd added sugar without asking, as well as a generous dash of milk. He was getting to know her more each day, what she liked and didn't like, her favourite foods, how she took her tea. It was scary and heartwarming. She wasn't sure which was the more defining emotion.

"Thanks," she said.

He winked at her. "I can't let you starve to death or dehydrate."

"I'm capable of hobbling into the kitchen to make myself a cup of tea. You really don't have to put yourself out like this. I'm not a complete invalid."

"It's not putting myself out at all," he said. He took her cup, set it on the table, then leaned in to gently kiss her lips. His own moved softly against hers as her pulse accelerated and heat flushed her cheeks.

Then he gazed down at her with a depth of emotion in his eyes that made her slightly uncomfortable, yet craving more. "You're quite a knight in shining armour. I would never have known."

He reached for the remote, the connection broken. "There's a lot you don't know about me."

"Is that so?"

He grunted in response.

"What should we watch?" she asked.

He flicked through the channels. "An action movie, a romantic comedy, a thriller? What are you in the mood for?"

"Romantic comedy," she replied, studying the outline of his face, the light stubble on his chin and cheeks, the way his hair stood on end where he'd run his fingers through it.

He selected a movie and got comfortable while she did her best to ignore the place on her foot that itched.

"It was nice to see you talking to your stepfather when we visited his house at Amity Point," she said.

"It was good to see him. It's been a while."

"I thought you hated him."

"Not hated, exactly. I suppose I did at the time — I was a teenaged boy with a stepfather laying down the law. He and my mum weren't getting along. In fact, they hadn't in years. I don't remember a time when they were happy together. They basically just lived their separate lives or fought, and there was nothing in between. I can see now that he was unhappy, and maybe he took that out on me. I was unhappy for my own unique reasons. I took that out on him and on anyone I could..."

"Like me?" Penny asked.

"Sometimes."

"That's the closest you've ever gotten to a genuine apology."

"I'm sorry if I hurt your feelings. I was hurting myself. My home life was chaotic. I had issues, and I dealt with them by teasing, taunting and generally causing mischief."

"You ran me over on your bicycle in front of the entire school and tore my skirt off on your handlebars. I ran home, crying, in my underwear. The entire student body saw my knickers, and I had scabs on my knees for weeks afterwards."

Rowan clamped his lips together. If he laughed, she was going to punch him. It might've happened thirty-five years earlier, but the humiliation she'd felt still stung a little.

He inhaled slowly. "I'm truly sorry about that. My brakes failed — I'd been working on them but I had to get to school, so I took a chance. I didn't see you in time to change course."

It was the first time he'd explained what'd happened. All these years, she'd assumed he'd run into her intentionally.

"You didn't do it on purpose?"

"I broke my wrist. You didn't know that?" He quirked an eyebrow as he rubbed his wrist reflexively.

"Really? I guess I thought that was from a football injury or something. I was so embarrassed that I ran right home. I didn't wait to see what'd happened to you."

"It was a painful experience for us both, I guess."

She reached out to rest a hand on his arm, then shifted closer so she could lay her head on his shoulder. "I'm sorry you broke your wrist."

"It's okay. It was a long time ago."

"And I'm sorry I blamed you for so long."

He put his arm around her shoulders and pulled her closer still. "Forget about it. It's all in the past. What matters is what happens now."

She met his gaze. Her pulse thudded, and she wondered how she'd missed seeing his kind heart all this time. She'd been so busy hating him that she'd forgotten the good things he'd done — like rescuing her and her friends from the rip at Point Prospect when they went swimming after a storm one afternoon. Or pulling her out of a mud puddle at the refuge.

"I suppose people can change, like your stepfather," she said.

"I really believed Buck was the enemy," he admitted. "But now I see he was just a man going through the hardest time of his life and not coping with it very well. I wasn't exactly an easy teenager to deal with, on top of his marriage problems. He lost his business around that time as well. And I recall some rumours going around about him being a serial killer or something. I didn't think much of it at the time—I was so caught up in my own pain and my anger at the world. But I'm sure that didn't help him cope with the situation."

Penny snuggled into Rowan's side. "And you've changed too. I'm glad I get to see the man you've become. You're all right, Rowan Clements."

"Oh, yeah?" He kissed the top of her head.

She tilted her face up, and his lips found hers, pressing gently at first, then searching hungrily for more. Her lips parted, and his tongue tested the way forward. She curled an arm around his neck as his hand moved to cup her cheek.

When he pulled back, his pupils were dilated. She smiled up at him, feeling warm all over.

"Maybe I can stay the night?" he asked, breathless.

"I don't want to rush things."

"Of course not," he agreed. "It's just that I'm leaving in a few weeks, and I want us to make the most of the time we have together."

"What? Where are you going?"

He studied her eyes, a smile teasing one corner of his mouth. "Why? Will you miss me?"

The look that'd always infuriated her in the past now seemed endearing. "Definitely — how long will you be gone?"

"I'm going to Israel on assignment for six weeks. It's a story we've been following for a while, and I've got to get the footage..."

"Israel? For six weeks?" she burst out.

"That's right — I travel a lot for my work. You know that."

She sighed. "I guess I thought maybe you'd stay ... now we're together."

He straightened in his seat. "But we're not serious or anything. I mean, it would be different if we were married. I'd try to get a job closer to home. But we're not."

She pulled away from him and crossed her arms over her chest. "Oh, really? We're not serious?"

He stood to his feet and gathered the teacups onto the tray. "You know what I mean."

"I'd love you to explain so maybe I can understand you better." She spat out the words, eyes flashing.

"I don't know..." He set down the tea tray and pressed both hands to his hips.

She stood to face him, hobbling forwards on her moon boot. "I'm feeling tired, Rowan. Perhaps you should go home."

He raised both hands, then let them drop to his sides. "Don't be like that, Pen."

"No, no... I wouldn't want to take up any more of your time, since we're not actually married. Maybe we should slow things down until there's a ring on it." She pointed to her ring finger.

He rolled his eyes. "Geesh, you can be dramatic sometimes."

"I'm dramatic now? Okay, it was lovely to see you, but you've got things to do, so I won't keep you." She ushered him towards the door, her moon boot thudding on the floorboards as she went. She opened the front door and pushed him out.

He leaned against the doorframe, lips pursed. "Give me a goodbye kiss, at least."

She pecked him on the lips, then shut the door in his face as she said, "Bye, buddy. Have a nice night."

She leaned against the door, laughter bubbled up inside her. After all the times he'd teased her over the years, he deserved that. Although she did feel a little bad about the kiss — she would've liked a better goodbye. But they could make up for it the next time she saw him. And perhaps he'd think about his priorities in the meantime.

She peeked out the small window beside the front door and saw him standing with his hands pressed to his hips. He kicked at a garden gnome on her porch, and it tumbled into the garden. Then he hurried down the steps and set the gnome right again before marching down the garden path to his car. He really was adorable.

Five

THE SAND GLINTED white under the hot sun. The ocean washed to shore with a sigh, blue and cool to the touch. Most weekend tourists had returned to the mainland. Blue Shoal was quiet. Taya splashed along the shoreline dressed in a red bikini with an enormous straw hat on her head. It was almost winter, but the heat on the island had hardly abated. It was still warm enough to swim, and Taya intended to make the most of it. Swimming in the ocean was one of her favourite pastimes.

"I don't know what to do," she said.

Beatrice, Eveleigh and Penny walked beside her. Penny's moon boot stuck out to one side. She'd covered it with a plastic bag for their walk, which Taya thought looked hilarious, although she wouldn't tell Penny so. Penny had injured her leg attempting to rescue an animal in remote bushland, then Rowan had found her and carried her to safety in his arms. It was a romantic story even if it had resulted in a broken bone for her friend.

Beatrice had brought Fudge, her pug, with her. The dog

was trotting along with them, tongue hanging out one side of his mouth.

"So, you're running out of money?" Bea asked.

"Not quite, but it's bound to happen if things keep going in this direction." Taya wrung her hands together.

"The new resort is the shiny thing right now," Penny said as they walked. "People like historical buildings. They enjoy the personal touch of your inn."

"I hope you're right," Taya replied, although her gut told her it wasn't true. She'd thought perhaps the downturn might last only a few weeks after the Paradise Resort opened, but now it'd been two months, and her bookings were lower than ever.

Evie was quiet. She was a businesswoman too. The look on her face said it all. "What do you think, Evie?"

Evie sighed. "Perhaps it's time to upgrade some things. Try to target the guests who want high-speed internet, a big-name chef, luxury appointments ... I don't know."

Taya considered her words. She might be right. But the panicked feeling in her gut made it difficult to concentrate on anything other than the fear that she'd fail. "I've definitely considered it. Do you think I should?"

"It's worth a try. You have to do something ... and my contractor is really great — he renovated my cottage and the cafe. I can give you his number," Bea said.

"Okay, thanks."

They strode along the sand to where their lounge chairs were set up, with beach towels and a picnic basket and an umbrella for shade. Taya lowered herself into a chair and removed her hat.

"If I don't take action to save my inn, it's going to fail or my father will buy it. One or the other."

"Would it be so bad if your dad owned it?" Bea asked, opening the picnic basket and setting the food on top of a towel. Crackers, cheeses of various types, a bowl of olives, dips and slices of crusty French bread.

"I don't know. Perhaps it's my inner child, but there's a part of me that rebels against the idea."

"So, you'll upgrade, and you'll fight to keep your business."

"And that horrid manager can forget about taking over," Taya added with a snort.

"What horrid manager?" Evie asked.

"Dad hired a manager for the resort. His name is Andrew, and he's so very smooth." She drew out the word on a wisp of breath.

Bea laughed. "That sounds like an insult."

"It is. I don't like smooth men. He dresses too perfectly, and his hair is just so." She mimicked his hairstyle with a swoop of one hand. "His teeth are white, his muscles are tight... I could write a poem about him." She giggled as she reached for an olive and popped it into her mouth.

"He sounds abominable," Bea quipped with a roll of her eyes.

"He is. And the worst of it is that he's so very nice about the idea of subsuming my business."

"Nice? Ugh." Penny chuckled.

"What you're telling us," Evie said, her brow furrowed, "is that he's handsome, athletic, well-dressed and nice?"

Taya's nostrils flared. "Well, when you put it that way, it sounds..."

"Like exactly the kind of man *you* need," Bea interrupted. "He's your type, Taya. You love well-dressed, handsome, kind men."

"Usually I do, but not this time. There's something so arrogant about him."

"But you said he's nice." Penny chewed on a cracker.

"Arrogantly nice," Taya corrected.

"You should ask him out," Bea said with a wink.

Taya gaped. "What? No. Definitely not."

"It's time you went on a date," Evie said.

Taya shook her head. "I'm perfectly content in my single life, thank you. And even if I wasn't, I wouldn't be interested in dating my father's employee."

The thought hadn't even crossed her mind. Andrew worked for her father; he wanted to ruin her life's work. The last thing on her mind was dating him. It was true that she hadn't been on a date in so long, she'd forgotten what it was like. But she'd come to terms with her life as it was, and she was happy enough.

Happy enough was fine. She didn't need bliss in order to enjoy her days. She could be perfectly content with a satisfying meal, a good day's work, a pleasant swim and a long run. Those were the things that brought her happiness, and she embraced them fully. They also wouldn't break her heart, and that was all she'd wanted after her husband died — to give her heart a break from the pain of loss. Loving someone new would disrupt her carefully planned and happy life. She had no desire to go there again.

* * *

Two weeks later, Taya had cancelled the few guests who had booked ahead, and the entire building was empty. She walked through the structure, watching the construction crew get to work sanding and prepping for painting.

Roofers were already climbing ladders and scaffolding to install a brand-new roof, and she had remodellers in the kitchen taking measurements. She'd decided to expand the kitchen so she could hire a head chef to coax their menu to the next level. She hoped it would spur greater numbers of guests to travel to the island. But if all her efforts failed, at least she could close the inn with a clear conscience, knowing that she'd done everything she could to save it.

By the time she made it outside, she was experiencing shortness of breath, dizziness and a pain in her side. So much change. So many aspects of the building would never be the same again once the contractor was done with it.

She sat on a mound of tiles and lowered her head as she attempted to calm her breathing. Panic attacks were something she'd experienced in her twenties, but it'd been at least a decade since her last one. It came on fast and lasted a few minutes. Finally her heart rate slowed, and the spinning in her head stopped. She'd been more and more anxious lately with everything that'd been happening with the inn. The worry was taking over her thoughts and her life. She'd lost the calm, contented existence that she'd built for herself years after her husband died and left her alone with the business to run and the mortgage to pay.

She gasped for breath, looking around. Thankfully no one had witnessed her display. The last thing she wanted was sympathy, or heaven forbid someone called the ambulance simply because she was in the throes of anxiety. She stood to her feet and smoothed down her skirt with one hand.

Her father's car pulled up the driveway, and he climbed out with a confused expression on his face.

"Hi, sweetie. What's going on here?" He wore a blue suit without a tie and tanned leather sandals. He walked towards her, slipping the sunglasses from his face to stare up at the inn.

"Hi, Dad. I decided to do some remodelling. Trying to get things back in shape so maybe my guests will stop leaving me for your fancy resort." She grimaced.

He embraced her and kissed the top of her head. "Good thinking, sweetie. I knew you'd come up with a plan."

She wiped the sweat from her forehead with the back of her sleeve. "I had to do something."

"Are you okay? You look a little pale." He cupped one hand beneath her chin and studied her face.

"I had a panic attack, that's all."

His brow furrowed. "That's not good. Why are you panicking?"

"This." She waved a hand at the building. "All of it. The guests leaving, the expenses cleaning out my bank account, the renovations doing damage to my savings. It's a lot to take on, and I'm a bit of a control freak, as you know."

"Oh, Taya, you can't hold so tight to things."

"That's easy for you to say. You've got a massive company with dozens of resorts to your name. This is all I have."

He shook his head, eyes narrowed. "This business is not *all* you have. You've got Camden, and you've got me and your mother. You've got your friends and your home. Even if this hotel shuts down tomorrow, you still have a full life with a lot of people who love you."

She sighed. "I know, but when Todd died, the inn was the only link I had left to him, other than Camden. I've held on to it so tightly because it was his legacy and mine."

"You're afraid if you let the past go, you'll lose the last connection you had with Todd?"

"We have our daughter, but she doesn't remember him..."

"This building doesn't either," Dad admonished gently as he put an arm around Taya's shoulders.

"I know, but it feels like it does. The paint colour we picked together, the grand piano in the entrance, the rug on the floor of the sitting room—there are bits and pieces of him everywhere. He helped build this place. When I'm here, I remember him better than I do anywhere else."

"Other than when you look in Camden's eyes, of course," Dad said with a wink.

"She does have Todd's eyes," Taya admitted.

"Sweetie, it's not healthy to be so connected to this place.

You don't know what the future holds, but if you equate maintaining a business with some kind of tribute to your deceased husband, you're going to set yourself up for heartbreak."

"You think I should sell?"

He faced her, head tipped to one side. "When was the last time you felt confident and happy running the business?"

She wrinkled her nose, pondering his words. "I can't remember."

He shook his head. "That's not a good thing, sweetie. You run a place like this because it's quaint and feeds a certain kind of lifestyle. If it doesn't do that, it's not worth all the headaches and expenses. You could do something else much easier."

"That's true," she admitted. "All I seem to do most days is work. If I'm not here running things, then I'm doing the accounts at night. It's a never-ending job."

"I'm not saying you should sell it, but at least try letting go emotionally so you don't find yourself in a panic over giving the place a face-lift."

"You're right, of course. But the problem is, I don't know how. I have no idea how to let go of this inn."

"What will be, will be," Dad said sagely.

She laughed. "That's so corny, Dad."

He huffed. "It's what dads do. We give corny advice."

She snuggled into his side and kissed his cheek. "Thanks, Dad. I really appreciate it."

Six

THE *SURF* *and Sea* restaurant was perched on the edge of the bay beside the ferry dock. Seagulls rested on the wings of the wind behind the building, scaling their way up on a warm breeze, then down again as they studied the seating to find an opening to dive for food.

Penny climbed out of Rowan's car, her moon boot clunking on the step as she lowered her feet to the ground. Rowan held the door open for her, then reached out to steady her steps. He was acting nervous and making her more so.

There was a band of sweat across his forehead. He wore a sports jacket over a buttoned white shirt and a pair of chinos. His hair was neatly combed to one side, and his cheeks were red. She wore a spaghetti strap blue-and-green chiffon dress with a flowing skirt that billowed around her legs as she walked. Her honey-blonde curls stuck to her neck, even though the day had turned cooler as the sun made its way towards the horizon.

"This is lovely," she said in an attempt to calm Rowan's nerves.

He grunted in response.

Why was he so nervous? They'd been out on dozens of dates since they first started seeing each other. Plus they'd known each other most of their lives.

The boot was due to come off the next day, and she couldn't be more excited about it. But she kept getting distracted from her joy at having dinner with her boyfriend in a restaurant she loved, and the impending freedom from the boot, by his strange behaviour.

He walked beside her in silence, his arm linked through hers to help her walk. Everything she'd said since he picked her up at home for their date had been met with either a blank stare or a grunt. Perhaps he was upset about something. She couldn't help thinking that his nervousness might not be a good sign. Surely he wouldn't take her to the nicest restaurant on the island for dinner only to end things between them.

The hostess showed them to their seats in the outdoors area. The sun hadn't fully set yet and hovered over the distant mainland, lighting up the still ocean in a vibrant display of yellow, pink and purple. A ferry chugged away from the island, and white water churned behind it. A man sailed by in a small boat, tugging at a rope to turn the direction of the sail.

Penny sat in her chair and straightened her dress while Rowan looked at his hands.

"Are you okay?" she asked.

"Yes, of course. Why do you ask?"

"You seem a little tense."

"No, not tense. I'm fine. How was your day?"

They chatted about mundane things — the animals she was tending, the grant money that'd come through and how she was using it to make a few changes to the refuge that would benefit all the animals.

She ordered fried snapper with *pommes frites* and steamed vegetables. He ordered a steak and prawn combination that looked teasingly delicious.

He talked about his upcoming trip to Israel and the preparations he and his colleagues were making as they did a deep dive, researching the story to give them all the information they needed to underpin their investigative piece.

She eyed his prawns.

"Do you want one?" he asked as he waved the crustacean around on his fork.

"I shouldn't... It's yours. I'm sure you want to eat it."

"I don't mind," he said.

"Then, yes, I'd love one. Thank you. They look amazing with all that butter sauce. I went for the healthy option, but I regret it now, seeing your meal."

"You should always order whatever you want," he said. "That's my motto. How often do you get to eat somewhere like this?"

He pushed his plate towards her, and she took a prawn and ate it. It was so soft, it practically melted in her mouth. Delicious butter, garlic and a hint of lemon — she closed her eyes to savour every bit.

"Wow, that was divine."

"We can swap meals, if you like."

"Really? You wouldn't mind?"

"I don't mind. It's worth it to see the look on your face."

They swapped plates. She felt bad about it for a few moments—until the first delectable bite of steak.

"You travel all over the world," she said after she'd swallowed her bite. "Surely you eat at much better restaurants than this all the time."

"I've been to a thousand amazing restaurants, but there's still nothing better than fresh-caught seafood on Coral Island."

After dinner, they ate chocolate pudding with fresh cream and drank brandy locally brewed on the mainland and made from mangoes. It was a little too sweet for Penny, but she was so caught up in the beauty and romance of the evening, she couldn't help exclaiming her approval over everything whether warranted or not. She was thankful that Rowan seemed to have relaxed—his nerves were less obvious at the very least. The reason for his tension still hadn't surfaced, but she'd forgotten about it by the time they reached his car and he opened the door for her.

He drove them to Point Prospect, where they climbed the few stairs to the lookout. The sun had well and truly set by then, and the ocean was an inky mass that surged below them, frothing white against the cliffs. A cool breeze lifted Penny's hair from her neck, and she nestled against Rowan's side as he curved an arm around her waist. She couldn't remember being so content. There was something so special about this man who felt like home and yet had been such a mystery to her over the years.

"I'm glad we've gotten the chance to spend so much time together lately," she whispered.

"It's been great," he agreed. Then he turned to face her, taking her hands in his. "I wanted to bring you here to tell you something. I've loved you for a long time. From a distance mostly, of course. Since you were so prickly around me. But I've known forever that you were the one for me. I kept coming back to the island whenever I had the chance, hoping you'd change your mind about me, but you never did. Until now."

She reached up on tippy-toe to kiss his lips. "I'm glad you persisted."

"Me too," he agreed. "And the reason I said we weren't serious the other night — I was trying not to scare you off."

"Mission accomplished." She sniffed.

"Sorry about that." He kissed her again, and she felt as though she might explode with happiness. "I didn't mean it — I'm very serious about you. In fact, we've wasted so many years being apart that I want us to start our lives together as soon as possible."

"I agree," she said. "I've been lonely all this time when I could've been with you."

His eyes glinted in the moonlight as he kissed the back of her hand. "That's why I think we should get married."

She blinked. "What?"

"I know it's quick, but I don't want to waste any more time. We've known each other our whole lives. We know the important things—the rest, we can take our time getting to know. But the main point is, I don't want to be apart. I don't want to spend weeks or months away on assignment without you. I don't want to come home to my tiny, very empty apartment. I want to be with you. Let's get married so we can be together always."

"I don't know. This is happening so fast," she said. Her heart hammered against her ribcage. Where had this come from? It was the last thing she'd expected. And yet something inside of her wanted to scream out *yes!* She'd never been married. Almost every one of her friends had married years earlier. Some were on their second marriage. She'd longed to know what it was like to have someone in her life who could be her partner in everything, to share every moment together. And Rowan was the best person she'd ever met—she knew that now. She'd misjudged him because of a childhood embarrassment, something she regretted deeply now that she knew his side of the story.

"Let's forget about being responsible just this one time. Let's be spontaneous and romantic and jump in with both feet. What do you say?"

She studied his face in the darkness. The glint in his eyes. The way the moon shone off his hair. The curve of his arms as they linked around her waist and pulled her close to him. The heat of his body as it warmed her. Then she looked up and caught his gaze. "Yes! Let's do it."

He laughed out loud and spun her around. Her dress flew out, and he held her off the ground as his lips descended over hers. Then he set her down again as his mouth explored every inch of her mouth, her neck.

"I love you," he whispered.

And she choked back tears as she said it to him in return. She'd finally found the man she could spend her life with, and she couldn't wait to start that life together.

Seven

BEATRICE'S FACE WAS HOT, sweat pooled beneath her armpits, and her hands shook slightly as she climbed into her father's boat and pushed off from the small dock in the bay below the house. She stood behind the wheel as the boat motored out of the bay and into the open ocean. Images ran through her mind as she rehearsed the words she'd say over and over again, imagining the various scenarios that could play out.

Once again, she asked herself if she was the right person to reveal the answer to her friend's long-held question. Penny's father had always been a secret. Penny's mother had refused to talk about him, wouldn't name him, had vowed to take the information about Penny's parentage to her grave. And yet, now that Beatrice knew the truth, she felt a heavy burden to share her newfound knowledge with Penny. Still, she'd seen her several times in the weeks since Betsy had told her about Buck building the cottage and Dad had revealed Buck was Penny's biological father, and she hadn't taken the opportunity to tell her friend.

None of the times they'd seen one another had been quite

right. There were other people around. That's what she told herself — it wouldn't be appropriate. Of course, she could've called Penny and set up a time. But she'd been so busy with the café and with Aidan now that they were dating again. Not to mention the time she spent with her father, making sure he was taking his medication, checking in on him, helping him around the house so he didn't exert himself too much — something he wasn't particularly happy about.

Now that she'd run through her list of excuses for the hundredth time, she imagined what Penny would say when she discovered that Bea had held on to the information for so long without saying a word. She sighed and adjusted the cap on her head as the wind buffeted it. Never mind, there was nothing she could do about it now. She couldn't travel back in time and choose a different course. She'd simply have to face her friend and tell the truth, whatever the consequences might be.

She pulled the boat into the small marina beside the wildlife refuge. The engine slowed to a chug, and the boat's wake settled into a pair of small waves breaking away on either side to disrupt the ocean's surface beneath the glittering sun.

June had brought with it the delightfully warm winter weather Coral Island was famous for — sunshine, sand and fun without the oppressive heat of summer. She steered the boat into the dock, stopped it and tied it in place, grabbed the picnic basket she'd prepared that morning and marched towards Penny's house.

They'd arranged to meet at Penny's for a light lunch. Bea thought it best that Penny be in the privacy of her home when she broke the news — who knew how her lifelong friend might react? She'd always been a little dramatic, and there could be a scene. Bea's pulse raced as she ran over again in her mind what her words should be — circumspect, rounding in on the point gently with a long, slow buildup? Or delving directly to the heart of the matter in one swift movement, like stripping off a Band-Aid? She couldn't decide. She'd have to figure it out when the moment came.

The sand was warm on her feet as it slipped between her toes. Her sandals were soon covered, and she leaned forwards to trudge faster. Driftwood had settled in a jagged line near the dunes, remnants of the storm they'd had last week. Beyond that, Penny's beach house nestled among the pandanus behind the dunes, looking warm and sleepy with half-shuttered windows like eyes and a smiling verandah for a mouth.

Potted plants were scattered along a sandy trail that led to the back steps. Bea climbed the steps, slipped off her sandals and knocked.

"There you are. I was about to send out a search party," Penny said as she opened the door.

Bea kissed her cheek and stepped inside. "I see the moon boot is gone. How does it feel?"

"Better. I'm like a new woman."

"That's good to hear. I brought a picnic, as promised, with your favourite dips and crusty bread."

"Perfect," Penny said, leading the way into the kitchen. "I'll get us some plates, and we can sit on the verandah and watch the surf."

They sat outside in two rocking chairs with a small table between them. The food was laid out on the table — sandwiches, crackers, cheese of various types, olives, dips and crusty bread. It was one of Penny's favourite meals. They'd always joked she could live on antipasto. Something Bea had begun to appreciate more as she got older — tasty, easy and ultimately satisfying.

Bea popped an olive into her mouth and squinted at the sparkling ocean. "The reason I wanted to catch up, just the two of us, is that I have something to talk to you about."

She faced Penny, who arched an eyebrow, chewing on a piece of bread.

Bea cleared her throat. This was harder than she'd thought it would be. Penny was so happy, carefree in the moment. Things between her and Rowan seemed to be good, as far as Bea could tell. She was glad her friend had found someone she could share her life with, and the refuge seemed to have recovered from imminent financial ruin. She hated to disrupt that contented look on her friend's face. But if she held on to this secret any longer, Penny would be furious with her — and rightly so.

"I had a conversation with Betsy recently..."

Penny swallowed. "How is she?"

"She's good. She had Samantha with her at the florist shop. Sam looked clean, happy and healthy. She was colouring."

"That's wonderful. I'm so glad they've reconnected." Penny's eyes gleamed as she reached for a cracker and sliced off a piece of camembert to set on top.

"She told me something." Best to do it quick, Bea decided in the moment. "She said it was Buck, Rowan's stepdad, who built the cottage — my beach cottage."

Penny gaped and set the cracker back down on her plate. "Wow. Really? That's... Well, I don't know what that is, but it seems big. Why didn't anyone tell us this before now?"

"It gets better, or at least more interesting." She wrung her hands together. "When I confronted Dad about it, he told me Buck is your biological father."

"What?" Penny's eyes narrowed. "No, that couldn't be right. He's Rowan's stepdad. He was married to June Clements when Mum was pregnant with me." She shook her head slowly back and forth. "How could he be my father? He's so much older than Mum."

Bea reached for Penny's hand and squeezed it gently. "It

was Buck Clements. I'm sorry, Penny. I know this is a lot to take in, and I didn't want to have to be the one to tell you. But it's true — Dad told me it was a big scandal. Buck had already married June when the truth came out. But he denied it, and most of the community backed him up. It was a different time back then—they didn't believe your mother or your grandmother."

Penny leaned back in her chair, staring out at the ocean. "I suppose it makes sense when you think about it. My parents never wanted to talk about it. If it'd been a boy from school, surely Mum would've just said so."

"It seems likely," Bea agreed.

"It was an adult man—that's why it was so hush-hush. And why they didn't want me to find out about it — they knew I'd be upset."

"I think that's probably true."

"I have to talk to Mum." Penny stood abruptly and tugged her mobile phone from her jeans pocket. She dialled and held it to her ear, then walked to the verandah steps and sat down. "Hi, Mum. I have to ask you something."

* * *

By the time Beatrice left her house, Penny's entire mind and body had gone numb. She should be angry, happy, sad, emotional—any number of reactions made sense given what Bea had told her. But she wasn't feeling anything much other than shock. What did it all mean?

Mum had confirmed the story through a barrage of tears and sobbing. "I'm sorry. I wanted to tell you, but I thought it would bring you too much pain. He's always denied you, never admitted you were his."

Penny understood then. Her mother had shielded her from the rejection she would've felt if she'd known as a child that her father lived on the island but didn't want to see her. It hurt as an adult to hear that—it would've devastated her as a child.

Her poor mother had carried that guilt and shame around all those years. Penny felt more sympathy for her than she ever had in her life before. She couldn't imagine what she'd do if she found herself in the same situation at forty-five, let alone as an sixteen-year-old girl.

A baby, with a married man, and the only one who believed her, a beloved mother, was murdered soon after. What a tragedy her young life had been. She shed a tear for her mother then, rather than for herself. She was an adult; she could handle the truth. But her poor mother had been through so much at such a tender age, her heart ached. If only she could go back in time and give her a hug. If only someone had.

When her grandmother was murdered, Mum was left to raise Penny alone in the beach house until Dad came along. It wasn't until that very moment that Penny realised how terrifying, lonely and isolating that time must've been for a teen mother in the 1970s. She'd call her back later, when Mum had a chance to calm down, and talk to her more about it.

One thing her mother had said before she hung up lingered in her mind as she got ready for bed. She climbed into the shower, her mother's voice ringing in her ear.

"Bea's mother, Luella, knew. She always believed me. But no one listened to her. They called her crazy. She was obsessed with bringing Buck to justice for what he did. She said he killed Mother too, although I can't believe him capable of that. She didn't think it was right for everyone to ignore me. I'll never forgive myself for telling her, getting her involved. She didn't have the strength to manage the pain of it the way I did."

Mum had carried that burden with her for so many years,

it had emerged as gasping sobs over the phone line. Finally, Dad had intervened and told Penny they could talk later. She heard his words of comfort as he took the phone from Mum and led her away before the line went dead. Penny's tears mingled with the shower water as she stood beneath the steady stream, letting it run hot over her head and down her back.

Buck Clements was her father. He was also Rowan's step-father. He'd seduced her mother when she was still a teen, maybe killed her grandmother and lived carefree on the island. She'd had tea with him in his living room. A shudder racked her body, and she opened her eyes wide. She had to do something about it.

Eight

TAYA STRODE through the inn's back door. The kitchen was hung with sheets; she couldn't see inside and preferred not to. Construction had begun in earnest, and since it was the weekend, there was no one on site. She hated to see the kitchen gutted and tools and cans of paint lying everywhere.

The girls had come over to help out while the construction crew were away. They'd agreed to paint the brand-new gazebo Taya had one of the local craftsmen erect in the garden. It saved a little money to paint it herself, so she'd told the man she'd do it. But she didn't realise just how much painting it would require and found herself dreading the task until Penny, Bea and Evie had offered to help. Now it was a party, and she was looking forward to their day together. She'd even ordered pizza to arrive at lunchtime and had made several litres of lemonade, using lemons from her garden, to get them through the morning.

She found her friends scattered about the gazebo. Beatrice sat beside one of the supporting beams, a paintbrush in hand. Penny stood on a stepladder on the other side of the structure and Evie surveyed the whole from a distance, hands shielding her eyes from the glare of the sun that set her red hair aflame.

"How does it look?" Taya asked, coming up alongside Evie.

Evie's hands dropped to her sides. "I love it. It's perfect for this space. I bet you'll have so many weddings here. I can picture it."

"I hope so," Taya said.

Penny climbed down from the ladder. "These intricate carvings around the edges are going to be hard to paint."

"If you have any ideas, I'm all ears."

"I guess we should try a smaller brush when we tackle them. Thankfully, the drop cloth will catch any drips." Penny nudged the cloth with a toe.

"I've never done much painting myself, so I'm counting on you ladies to help me out today." Taya strode over to where she'd laid out a series of paintbrushes and pots of paint to select her own.

Her brown hair was covered with a scarf and pulled into a ponytail. She wore an old pair of denim overalls and a stained white crop top. Her feet were bare, and she figured they'd be covered in paint by the end of the day. It was a small price to pay for the inn to be beautiful. She was pouring everything she had into the place. Her last-ditch effort to make it work.

"I've done more painting than I ever should have," Bea said as she ran the paintbrush over the woodwork. "Unfortunately, my ex-husband wasn't much of a painter. Or a cleaner. Or a cook or landscaper, for that matter." She laughed. "Now that it's all out in the open, it seems he wasn't much of a husband either. All those years, I excused his lack of contribution around the house with things like, 'Oh, but he's such a good husband and father, and he works so hard...'"

Penny shook her head as she carried a paintbrush and tin

up the ladder again. "I hope my marriage doesn't go the same way…"

Taya's brow furrowed. "What marriage?" She popped the lid off a tin of paint and began to stir.

Penny's cheeks reddened. She studied the paintbrush in her hand and dipped it quickly into the paint before running it over a section of timber.

"What's going on, Pen?" Evie asked, her eyes narrowed. "Your face is on fire, which means you're embarrassed or upset about something. It's always been like that. Even in high school, I could tell when something was up, because of those cheeks."

Penny set the tin and brush on the top rung of the ladder and climbed back down. "I have news to tell you all."

"Okay." Taya straightened and gave Penny her full attention.

Bea stopped painting. Evie pressed both hands to her hips.

Penny tugged off her gloves and pushed out a hand, displaying a thin gold ring with a blue stone in the centre. "I'm engaged!"

Taya gaped.

Beatrice grinned.

Evie exclaimed aloud and rushed to embrace her friend.

"Engaged?" Taya asked, her brain fuzzy as she attempted to process Penny's words. Penny had never been engaged before. Never married. She'd always been Taya's single friend. The one she could call whenever anything went wrong in her life or she needed help. She'd counted on Penny always being there for her, that they'd grow old together, just the two of them, and could take long walks on the beach or through the town with their walking sticks when the sand became too difficult to navigate. They'd shout the latest gossip at each other when their hearing deteriorated, and they'd attend water aerobics classes at the local pool. How could she be engaged? If Penny got married, it'd change everything.

"Rowan asked and I said yes."

"I'm so happy for you." Taya hurried to give Penny a hug, but inside was a ball of nerves that tumbled about her stomach. Everything was changing. "Congratulations, honey."

Evie jumped up and down, clapping her hands together in excitement. "We're going to have a wedding! I've been hoping for this day for so long."

"Settle down." Penny laughed. "It's really not a big deal."

"Not a big deal?" Bea asked, embracing Penny. "It's a very big deal. You're joining your life with another person. Everything will be different."

"Well, not everything..." Penny's eyebrows drew together. "Right?"

"Yep, everything," Taya agreed.

"I'll still live here on the island in my beach house and run my wildlife refuge. I'll still be friends with all of you and see you regularly. Those things won't change."

"As far as you know," Bea said. "But once you're married, you may find you have to move for Rowan's work."

"I don't know about that..." Penny's cheeks grew warmer by the moment. She fussed with her hair. "We've talked about it, and he knows how much I love it here. He says he's willing to give up journalism."

"It's all very sudden. Are you sure about this?" Taya studied her friend's face. There was joy in her eyes, but an element of fear as well.

"I think so..." Penny chewed on her lower lip. "I mean, I should be certain. Shouldn't I? Maybe that's a sign. If I'm not completely sure, one hundred percent, that I should marry him, maybe I shouldn't. I don't know. It's very quick, but then again, we've known each other forever."

Beatrice took Penny's hands in hers and squeezed them. "Don't listen to us. Can you imagine growing old with him?"

"Definitely."

"Would you want to grow old without him?"

"No." Penny blinked a few times. "I can't even think about living without him. I want to be with him all the time."

"That sounds like love to me," Evie said. "Not that I've been very lucky in love, but I recognise it when I see it."

"Don't let us talk you out of it," Taya added. "But maybe you should have some of those kinds of discussions with Rowan — where you'll live, how you'll live. What about bank accounts—will you have a joint account or separate? Do you want kids? All those kinds of things are important to talk about."

"Kids?" Penny asked, one eyebrow quirked. "Unless we adopt, that's not likely to happen, as much as I would've loved to be a mother. So I'm not sure that's a conversation we should have."

"Taya's right. You need to talk about it with Rowan, even if you assume you're on the same page. You could be wrong, and whatever it is might end up being a deal breaker for one or both of you."

"Did you talk about those things with Preston before you were married?"

"Nope," Bea replied. "We were so young. And look how that turned out."

* * *

Finally, white paint covered the entire gazebo, and all four of the women were exhausted. They cleaned out their brushes and sat in lawn chairs in the shade to drink lemonade and pizza as they enjoyed their view over Blue Shoal Beach.

"You have white paint on your nose," Evie said with a giggle, pointing at Taya's face.

Taya gulped down lemonade. "I'm sure it will come off in the shower."

"Um..." Bea said.

"Really?" Taya asked. "It won't come off?"

"You may have a white nose for a little while." Evie reached for a piece of cinnamon tea cake that Beatrice had brought with her. "It's in my hair too, so I'll look as though I have grey streaks for a few days."

"Speaking of grey streaks," Bea said. "I found several grey hairs this morning when I looked in the mirror. It's getting worse. I can't keep plucking them out or I'll go bald."

"Embrace it," Taya said. "That's what I plan on doing. I think you'll look lovely with grey hair."

"I don't know about that," Bea replied.

"Who is that coming towards us?" Penny asked around a mouthful of cake. She pointed down the beach at a figure dressed in jeans and a white T-shirt striding in their direction.

Taya's heart skipped a beat. "It's that man I told you about, Andrew. Ugh — what does he want now?"

Andrew climbed the stairs from the beach to the lawn and tipped his hat at them. "Good morning, ladies. How are you all on this fine day?"

"We're well, thank you," Taya replied.

His eyes were hidden by a pair of dark sunglasses. "I see you've begun the renovations on the inn. How's it going?"

"Perfectly well, thank you. I couldn't be happier with our progress. It was time for an update, and I think it will be just what our guests need to make their stay even more enjoyable."

Bea arched an eyebrow at Taya. Evie bit down on her lower lip as if to stifle a laugh. Taya did her best to ignore them. She had no idea what they found so amusing, but she was not going to embarrass herself in front of Andrew. It was bad enough that he could tell the resort had pushed her to upgrade her inn. She didn't want him to know how dire things had become.

"That's good to hear."

"These are my friends." She introduced Andrew to the other ladies, and he was distracted for several minutes making polite chitchat with each of them in turn. He really was charming, she had to admit. Before long, her friends were smiling and laughing, telling him all about themselves, fawning over the photographs in his wallet of his nieces and nephews and asking him questions about his life. She stayed seated where she was while they crowded around him. She let her eyes drift shut so she could block out the sight and instead imagined she was standing on the headland, alone, staring out at the horizon as gulls circled overhead. There was no stress, no inn to manage, no employees to pay, no profit to make and no responsibilities to carry. She was free, and her shoulders were light.

"Can I speak to you a moment?" Andrew's voice brought her back to reality with a jolt.

Her eyes blinked open, and she found him staring down at her, his sunglasses in his hand and his brown eyes fixed on her.

She stood to her feet. "I'll be back in a few moments."

She led him around the outside of the inn to the rose garden and took a seat on a bench beneath a canopy of climbing roses. He sat beside her.

"It feels good to sit. It's been a busy day."

"I'm sure it has. How can I help you, Andrew?"

He caught her gaze. "You're so formal with me."

"Am I?"

"Yes, you are. Are you like this with everyone?"

"I don't know what you mean."

"Did I offend you somehow?"

"Do you recall the first time we met?"

"At your parents'?"

"No, when you thought I was a guest here at the inn."

"Oh right, that. Of course I remember. I thought you were a beautiful visitor who'd travelled to the island to relax. You looked so happy, so carefree."

She grunted. "I was neither relaxed nor carefree, so I guess the joke is on you."

"Has the extremely composed Taya Eldridge just cracked a joke?" He laughed.

"I'm not as repressed as you imagine."

"I don't imagine any such thing."

"Is there a reason you had the sudden need to talk to me in private? I'm neglecting my friends."

"Right," he replied, leaning forwards. "When I saw you that first time, I insinuated that I'd like to buy this inn."

"I know," she said. "Your true intentions were laid bare."

"It's not a secret." He linked his hands together, elbows on his thighs. "Your father told me to keep an eye out for opportunities to expand our offerings in Blue Shoal. I think your hotel would be a valuable addition for our guests who want a more historical experience, but would still like to be able to access the many services and comforts of the Paradise Resort."

"I'm sure you believe that."

"I didn't know you were an Eldridge."

"Well... I am. What difference does it make?"

He shifted uncomfortably on the bench. "Don't you see? It makes all the difference. Why not join with us? We can merge the two businesses, and you can reduce your overhead and your stress levels. You can manage the place but have the cash behind you to transform it into the kind of getaway you've always dreamed of."

She pushed out her chin. "I'm already turning it into the kind of getaway I've always dreamed of."

"That's great, and I applaud you for it. But think about it

— okay. I've spoken to your father, he's on board. This is an offer — we'd like to buy your business, make it part of the Eldridge family holdings, and give you a chance to finally take some time off. Time for yourself. Maybe you could travel, or have a spa day, or do something to relax. We'd hire an assistant manager to support you so you'd have the flexibility for a life of your own. You'd still get to make the decisions, in consultation with your father, on the direction you take the business. But you'd have backup."

Taya didn't know what to say. A part of her felt defensive about what she'd built. How dare he insinuate she hadn't done a good-enough job of making her inn a must-see destination? But at the same time, something deep inside her pined for the chance to relax, to pull back and let someone else carry the burden of the place for a while. It was hard to run a business alone. There was never an opportunity to leave, even for a few days. Things went wrong, staff called in sick, pipes burst, and in the end, she rarely got the chance for more than a day or two off in a row.

She hadn't taken a decent holiday in two decades. She'd love the chance to stay with her daughter in Cairns and see the sights, but she couldn't manage the time off. Maybe this wasn't such a terrible idea. But it was Andrew; he was out to destroy everything she'd built. She could tell by the look on his oh-so-innocent and handsome face. The offer was too good to be true. And besides that, she'd sworn she'd never sell her inn. It was a part of her. A connection to her marriage and her grief, her motherhood and her joy. It'd always been there with her, through the good times and bad. It'd provided the income she needed to raise a daughter alone and to keep busy when she thought she might be swallowed by the grief over losing her husband.

Could she do something so drastic at this time in her life?

Nine

THE COTTAGE WAS noisy and full again, and Beatrice couldn't be happier. She loved it when the children came to stay, though she wasn't sure she could call them children any longer since both of them had passed the age of eighteen. Harry was nineteen now and looked it — he had a tiny amount of dark stubble around his mouth. His long hair brushed against his shoulders — curly and unruly. He was tall, lanky, and had dark smudges beneath his eyes. In fact, he looked even thinner than usual. She hoped he wasn't partying too hard.

"You know, you've got to keep up with your studies," she said to him as she buttered a piece of toast for his breakfast.

"I know, Mum. I study plenty." He slipped a piece of crust to Fudge, who stood panting beneath the table, waiting.

"Maybe you're staying up too late, though."

He frowned. "What are you talking about?"

"You look tired."

"Gee, thanks."

"I mean it. You're nineteen years old—you shouldn't look tired. You should be able to manage on very little sleep. What's going on? You're not into anything you shouldn't be, are you?"

He rolled his eyes as she handed him the toast with a generous portion of melted butter and Vegemite spread thin over the top, just the way he liked it. "No, Mum. I'm doing everything I should do and nothing I shouldn't."

"Now you're placating me."

"Maybe." He chuckled and took a bite of toast. "Although I have to admit, I've been a bit of an insomniac lately for some reason."

"Oh, no. Maybe we should take you to the doctor or the naturopath. I had a good one in the Sydney CBD. I can look up her number for you."

"Thanks, Mum. I'm sure I'm fine. I just need to get some sleep. I think two weeks on the island should do the trick. I'm looking forward to lots of lying about, swimming and eating."

"You're skinny, too. I'll make you some lasagne for dinner tonight."

"Perfect. I've been aching to come home and eat some of your cooking. Nothing tastes as good these days. The cafeteria at the university keeps repeating the same recipes, and I'm kind of sick of them, honestly. I miss your food."

"I'm glad you miss me for something," she quipped, sitting at the table beside him with a wink.

She sipped her tea. Dani emerged from the bedroom with a towel wrapped around her wet hair. She'd cut it much shorter so it settled just below her chin in a bob. In comparison with her brother, she looked well rested, happy and healthy. She poured cereal into a bowl and added milk before eating hungrily.

"It's good to be home."

"I'm glad you're here," Bea said. "There's so much I want to talk to you about, but I'll give you a chance to catch your breath first."

Dani spoke around a mouthful of muesli. "We've got some things to tell you as well."

"Oh?" Bea sipped her hot tea.

"Dad has moved back into our old neighbourhood with Annie Draper," Dani said, watching Bea's reaction with compassion in her eyes.

Bea stifled a flash of anger. "I suppose that was inevitable. Annie always loved it there, she wasn't likely to leave for Melbourne. But I didn't realise they were living together."

"Yep. He's moved into Annie's house. Her kids are off at university, of course, the divorce with her husband has been finalised. And Dad had nowhere to stay."

"So it made sense, I suppose." Bea's nostrils flared. How could Preston do it? There were millions of women in the country he could date, but he had to choose one of her friends. And to top it off, the two of them would live in the same neighbourhood they'd raised their family in. "No doubt they're spending time with all our old social circle."

"They've joined the golf club. They're part of that book club you used to attend. And I know they went out to dinner with the Fosters the other night."

"How strange," Bea said. "It's like he's simply replaced me with a different model."

"Don't say that, Mum," Harry said. "It's not like that. He's fallen in love—that's all. Kind of like you and Aidan."

"I suppose you're right." Bea sighed. "I shouldn't judge so harshly. Although it happened very quickly, considering he wanted to marry Geri not so long ago."

The two kids exchanged an uncomfortable look. She didn't want to be that mother — the one who criticised their father in front of them. It would do nothing but cause friction and division in the family. They'd stop telling her things, or they'd defend him and push her away. Her overwhelming desire was for them all to be able to get along and continue to be a family, regardless of the direction Preston took his love life. She wanted to be regally poised and perfectly gracious, and say things like *Well, isn't that lovely, I wish them nothing but the best.* But she couldn't do it, at least not yet. She'd work on being a better person just as soon as the shock wore off.

"I'm sorry. I don't mean to be that way. It pops out sometimes. You know I want the best for your dad and ... whoever he's dating."

Dani reached for her hand and squeezed it. "It's okay, Mum. We understand. We love you and want you to be happy."

"And I adore you both for that." She patted Dani's hand. "Now, who wants a tea or coffee?"

* * *

An hour later, Harry had gone back to bed. Bea tried to recall what it was like as a teen, being able to sleep at will for most of the day, and failed. Aches in her back got her up and out of bed most mornings if she ever had the luxury of sleeping in. Generally that only happened on a Monday now that she owned the café and had to open up at an early hour every morning.

Dani trudged up the hill to visit her grandfather. She'd decided to take up photography as a hobby after Bea gave her an SLR camera for Christmas, and her grandfather had promised to drive her to some scenic locations.

Bea had just sat down with a book to enjoy a few moments of relaxation when she heard tyres on the gravel driveway. She stepped outside and tented a hand over her eyes. Aidan climbed out of his truck with a wave. A thrill of anticipation ran through her. She jogged to meet him and threw her arms around his neck, feeling like a schoolgirl all over again. It was exciting to be in love, and even more so with her high school sweetheart. She could never have imagined this might be a possibility throughout the lonely last years of her marriage with Preston.

"Well, this is a nice greeting," Aidan said after she kissed him on the lips.

She laughed. "I'm glad to see you. That's all."

"I'll have to surprise you more often." He looped his arms around her back and held her close. "What are you up to?"

"Harry's sleeping, Dani's out taking photos on her new camera with Dad, and I'm on my own."

"Want to take a walk?"

"I'd love to. Let me grab my hat."

They strolled along the beach she thought of as her own, since it was rare that anyone else ever stumbled across it. The only access point was past her cottage or at the other end over a rocky outcropping. Every now and then, a few ambitious swimmers came to try out the waves at the end of the beach around the rocks and the reef, but otherwise, she had the place to herself. It was peaceful and serene, and one of her favourite places in the whole world. She spent many morning hours striding along it, thinking about life and imagining her future.

Aidan reached for her hand, and the warmth of his touch reminded her of everything she was grateful for. She didn't mind that Preston had moved in with Annie, was living in their old neighbourhood again and spending time with all their old friends. She didn't want that life any longer. She'd left it all behind and had barely given it a second thought.

Moving back to Coral Island was the best decision she'd made in a long time. She loved her little beach cottage and the life she'd built there. Living so close to her father was a big bonus — the fact that she could see him every day with very little effort gave her such a sense of contentment that it was difficult for her to imagine ever leaving. They'd reconnected and felt completely comfortable around one another again.

Her main regret was that she'd let things slip between them for so long, not giving him the attention she should've while she lived in Sydney. But she was making up for lost time with him and her brother, Bradford, now.

Aidan was the cherry on top. Even when they were apart, she was satisfied with the changes she'd made. But now that they were back together, she was truly happy.

"Grace is coming to visit next week," he said.

"That will be nice. Dani and Harry might get a chance to meet her."

"I hoped you'd be okay with that."

"Of course. I think it's a great idea."

"Good. I've got so many things planned. I want to take her snorkelling, but I thought maybe you could all join us too. It's a lot more fun with a bigger group."

"That sounds perfect," Bea replied.

"Also, maybe we could all have dinner together."

"We'd love that."

He pulled her hand to his mouth to kiss the back of it as they walked. "I'm looking forward to seeing her again. This time, it's with her mother's blessing, so I think I'll enjoy it a lot more."

"You'll find your rhythm. You're a good father already, Aidan."

"I hope so. I've missed too much of her life. So many things I wish I'd been there to witness, to be part of. But I'm trying to let go of those regrets and appreciate the moment."

"I think that's wise. None of us can travel back in time and change things, no matter how much we'd like to. And hopefully the two of you will experience many decades of life together."

"It's crazy to think of myself as a dad. I truly never believed it would happen."

"I'm happy for you. I'm especially happy that I can share it with you."

He stopped walking and faced her, cupping her cheeks with his hands. "I'm sorry I pushed you away. I tend to do that when I'm feeling overwhelmed. But I want us to be together always — this isn't a short term thing for me."

She swallowed around a lump in her throat at his words. That was what she wanted too, but she couldn't bring herself to express it. Instead, she simply nodded. He kissed her.

Then they walked back to the cottage together, her heart full.

Ten

THE CAFÉ WAS busy with the burst of tourists that always accompanied the beginning of the school holidays. Dani had offered to come and help out, which Bea was grateful for. Between the few staff members she'd managed to train so far and their tendency to flake out at the last moment, calling in sick or coming in late with excuses like they fell and had to minister to their knees, or they were on their period, or they stayed up too late drinking and overslept, she was struggling to keep up.

She also wondered if the younger generation was going to make it until she witnessed her beautiful daughter waiting tables, smiling at customers and working hard without a break for hours at a time.

When finally there was a break in the crowd for a few minutes, she insisted that Dani take a seat at a small table by the window with her. The two of them sipped on cups of iced tea and shared a slice of carrot cake. Bea thrust her fork into the cake and pulled away a chunk of the moist, flavourful dessert, popping it into her mouth before it could fall.

"Is it always this busy?" Dani asked around a mouthful.

"No, this is the holiday rush, but it's often pretty busy. I can keep up with it fairly well, though. Thankfully, the part-timers help out. But I can't always rely on them."

Two of her staff had showed up that morning and were busily restocking the trays in the display cabinet and filling orders.

"I wish I could be here to help you more often, Mum. This is a lot for you to take on alone."

"I'm not alone. I've got help. And I'm managing okay."

"You should see if you can hire someone full-time to give you a bit more support."

Bea had thought of that, but she'd shied away from it. Managing the few part-time staff she had was hard enough. She hated the idea of bringing on any full-time staff. She'd never managed people before, and the prospect was daunting.

"I don't know..."

"You need it, Mum. What if you want to go away for a weekend or for longer — a holiday to Thailand or something? You've got to be able to take a break. It's crazy how many hours you put into this place."

"Maybe you're right," Bea said. "I am feeling pretty tired."

"I'm exhausted after half a shift." Dani laughed. "I can't imagine how you feel."

Just then, Evie strode across the café and sat down across from Bea. "I'm here. Sorry, I got caught up with customers. They're all eating at the café and then migrating into the book-shop to browse."

"It seems to be working well," Bea said.

Evie nodded, her red curls bobbing around her porcelain face, green eyes wide. "Exactly how I'd hoped it would. Your café is brilliant, Bea. I'm so glad you agreed to do it. I love it here. It's become one of my favourite places to visit on the island."

"I'm glad. Me too," Bea replied. "Now, wait right there,

I'm going to get you some cake. This one turned out pretty well, if I do say so myself."

"It's divine," Dani admitted, taking another bite.

By the time Bea returned with a pitcher of iced tea, glasses stacked together and several more slices of cake, the other women had arrived. Taya and Penny were chattering about the renovations on the inn, Evie was listening as she chewed on a fingernail, and Dani was finishing her slice of cake.

"Good morning," Bea said as she set everything out on the table. "Tea and cake all round."

They exclaimed in delight and reached for a glass and a plate of cake. For a few moments, there wasn't as much talking as they got organised. Then Bea lifted her purse off the floor and set it on the table. "I asked you all here because I wanted to show you something."

She pulled out a folder and set it on the table, her purse back on the floor. "As we previously agreed, I've continued questioning people around the community, when I could, about the murder of Mary Brown, Penny's grandmother. I went to the police station a few days ago and asked for the case files, and they gave me this."

She tugged a piece of paper out of the folder and held it aloft. "As you can see, they've redacted a lot of the content, and they didn't give me much. They were fairly reluctant even to hand this over. Much of what's on this sheet, we already knew. It gives information about Mary, who she was, where she lived, how she died — which was by strangulation."

"Oh, I didn't know that," Dani said, her brown eyes wide.

"Sorry, honey, you don't have to stay for this if you don't want to," Bea said, placing a hand over her daughter's.

"No, I want to. It's intriguing. I can't believe you're all investigating this cold case — you're like Sherlock Holmes or something."

"Not sure we're quite that accomplished," Taya replied.

"Go on, Beatrice. What were you saying?" Penny piped up.

Bea cleared her throat. "Yes, thanks, Pen. Okay, I was saying — it says here the suspect, a Buck Clements, was cleared of any wrongdoing because of an alibi."

"What was the alibi?" Evie asked as she set down her tea glass.

"His alibi was given by Betsy Norton."

Taya gasped. Evie's brow furrowed.

Penny leaned back in her chair, hands pressed to her forehead. "What? Really? That seems like something she would've told us."

"I suppose we didn't ask her about it," Bea said. She wanted to give her new friend the benefit of the doubt. Betsy was old. Maybe she was confused, or perhaps it hadn't crossed her mind to talk about the alibi. "And besides, she might not remember much about it. After all, it happened a long time ago. Let's not forget that."

"So, what did she say? What was her alibi?"

"They went fishing together," Bea said.

* * *

A few minutes later, the topic of conversation changed to wedding plans.

"Where will you get married?" Evie asked.

"I thought we might stand on the beach at Blue Shoal and have the reception at Taya's inn."

Taya blinked. "Oh, that would be wonderful. But I'm not sure when the renovations will be complete. It could be months."

"That's okay," Penny said. "We don't mind waiting."

"Have you set a date yet?" Taya asked.

Penny helped clear the empty plates from the table. "We

don't have a date, but we'd like something in autumn. Do you think the remodel will be done by then?"

"It certainly should be. I'll go out of business if it takes longer than nine months to do a simple face-lift." She laughed, but the sound was hollow.

Bea wondered how long Taya's finances could hold out, but she didn't want to pry.

"Actually, there was something I wanted to talk to you all about. I'd love you to be my bridesmaids."

Bea's throat tightened. She couldn't be happier for her friend. She'd been a bridesmaid once before, in her twenties. But not since. This was a special moment. "Oh, wow. That's lovely."

"Of course we will," Taya said, wiping her eyes with the corner of a napkin.

Evie threw her arms around Penny. "How exciting!"

Penny's eyes glistened as Evie released her. "I wouldn't want anyone else to do it. I'm glad all of you are on the island and can share this with me."

"Me too," Bea replied. "It's going to be such fun."

"Will you be my matron of honour, Taya?" Penny asked.

Taya's cheeks pinked. She wiped her eyes again and cleared her throat. "I'd love to. Thank you."

She leaned in to hug Penny. Bea wanted to cry as well. There were sniffles all around the table. Even Dani had to hurry away wiping her eyes to serve a customer.

The doorbell chimed, and Betsy came in. She closed her umbrella and shook off water droplets in the entryway, then wiped her feet on the mat before glancing at the women.

"Will you look at that?" Bea exclaimed. "It's raining, and we didn't even notice."

Rain bucketed down then, soaking the small village and obscuring it from view through the nearby window within seconds. The sound drowned out the noise of conversation and the hum of the coffee machine. Betsy shuffled over to their table.

She wore a purple tunic with red and pink flowers printed all over it, along with a chunky gold chain around her pale, lined neck.

"What's going on here? Looks like you're having quite the party." She grinned.

Bea pulled a chair out for her. "Would you like to join us, Betsy? We're talking wedding plans. Penny and Rowan got engaged."

Betsy's eyebrows arched sky-high. "Well, that's wonderful news. Congratulations, honey. The two of you make a very handsome couple." She sat beside Bea with a grunt. "It feels good to get off my feet. I've been buzzing all over town running errands on my lunch break when it started to rain. This was the nearest place I could escape to, and I thought a hot coffee might be nice."

"I'll get you one," Bea said, jumping to her feet. "I've got sandwiches set aside for the group too. Cake first, sandwiches second — the best way to live."

She hurried off to get the sandwiches and coffee. When she returned, Penny was setting an appointment time with Betsy to pick out the flowers for the wedding.

"But we don't have a date yet," she said.

"It don't matter, honey. You come in and make your selection. Then, when you have a date, you let me know. We'll work it out."

Bea set the plate of sandwiches, chips and pickles in the middle of the table and cleared the last of the cake plates. She returned from the counter with Betsy's coffee along with a refill of iced tea.

"What did I miss?"

"We asked Betsy about the police report," Taya said with a dip of her head in the older lady's direction.

Bea sat in her chair, interest piqued. She'd wanted to ask Betsy about the report, but she wasn't sure how to raise the subject. "That's right — you told me Buck built my cottage and that you saw my mother go in—that's when she dropped the music box you found. But you never mentioned being his alibi for the time of the murder."

Betsy cocked her head to one side. "Now let me see... I guess I didn't. I don't know what I said or didn't say these days. I can't recall. But I'm glad you girls are on top of it. The report is correct—I was with Buck that day. I'm trying to remember what we were doing. I think we were fishing at my secret fishing hole." She tapped a finger alongside her nose and shot Bea a pointed look.

She had no intention of sharing the location of Betsy's favourite hideaway with anyone. Nor did she think they'd care or be interested even if she did. Betsy was a quirky character, but that's what Bea had grown to love about her.

"I suppose that makes sense," Penny said quietly.

Bea chewed on the inside of her cheek. "I didn't realise you and Buck were friends. Although I suppose two Americans on an island off the coast of Queensland would probably find each other quickly enough."

"Well, you can say that, I suppose. Although we've known each other since the day he arrived on the earth."

Evie frowned. "What...?"

"Don't you girls know? Didn't your father tell you, honey?" She peered at Bea through widened eyes. "My maiden name was Clements — Buck is my brother."

Eleven

THE LIPSTICK WAS CORAL PINK, and as Bea smoothed it across her lips, she noticed it had a crack in one side and the stick was slanted, as though it might collapse at any moment. She frowned in frustration — it was brand new. How irritating. She didn't visit the mainland often these days, so finding her favourite brand of lipstick had become a chore unless she chose to shop online.

She didn't want to buy everything on the internet. She preferred to visit a store and pick out the things she liked, with the personal touch of a customer service representative there to help her. But she wasn't sure how soon she could visit Airlie Beach again and sighed with resignation over the realisation that she'd have to shop online more often if she was going to live on Coral Island.

As she finished applying her makeup, she thought about what Betsy had revealed to them the day prior in the café. She'd hurried back to her flower shop the moment the rain had stopped, leaving the four women in stunned silence behind her. They'd quickly regained their senses and discussed in hushed tones what it might mean. They hadn't gotten far with it, though, since the café grew busy again and the other three women had businesses to return to as well. But it'd been on Bea's mind ever since.

Did it matter that Betsy was Buck's sister? The police had dropped the charges against him, so the evidence clearly wasn't there to convict him. Also, the man Bea met was lovely, welcoming, elderly and a gardener — gardeners couldn't hurt a fly. Could they?

It was all very confusing. Something that'd happened so long ago — how could any of them figure out what the police had never managed to solve?

There was a knock at her front door. She shouted from the bathroom that the door was open, then hurried to finish dressing.

Bradford waited in the kitchen, sipping a glass of home-squeezed lemonade she'd made the day before. "This is great," he said, taking a giant gulp. "Anything to eat?" He opened the pantry and nosed around.

She laughed and pulled out a container of brownies. "Here you go. We can take them with us. Eat as many as you like. Harry's hardly emerged from his bedroom and isn't eating much at all. I made them for him, but they'll go bad if someone doesn't eat them."

"Is he sick?" Brad asked as he took out a brownie and snapped the lid shut before tucking the container beneath his arm.

"He seems to have caught something. Although I'm a little worried because he's not bouncing back the way he should. I've made him a doctor's appointment for this afternoon. It's probably nothing, but I'll feel better knowing for certain."

"Let me know how it goes. He's young and fit—he shouldn't be lying in bed all the time."

"Apparently it's what teenaged boys do," Bea said.

"So, are you ready to find the boat of your dreams?"

Bea laughed. "I don't know if I can afford that. But something that won't sink will suit me just fine."

"Let's go, then."

Bradford drove them down to the marina. Bea had decided when she moved back to Coral Island that she'd buy a boat instead of a car. Dad said she could continue driving his old station wagon since he had a truck he used most of the time anyway. And to get to Blue Shoal or Point Prospect, it was faster and more enjoyable for Bea to take the ocean rather than the road. A small boat with an inboard motor and centre console with a shade was exactly what she needed. Besides, it would be fun to take the kids out fishing or snorkelling while they were home for the holidays.

It was an overcast day. Grey clouds hung low over the island.

"We'll have to be quick," Bradford said, eying the sky. "The weather could turn at any moment."

It was low tide. Boats around the marina sat moored to docks in the stormy water. Bea always marvelled at the way the ocean changed according to the weather — sometimes crystal clear, sometimes deep blue and at other times a murky grey.

They checked the notice board first and tugged a few phone numbers from sheets of tear-off slips. Bea carried them in one hand while they toured the marina, looking at boats. She made mental notes about what she wanted and didn't want in a boat as they went. They spied one with a "for sale" sign posted in the front window. It looked like the type of thing she was after — small, with a centre console, partial roof for shade and an inboard motor. It was an older model, with some signs of wear and tear, but seemed in decent shape at first glance.

"Let's call the number," Brad said.

He dialled on his mobile phone and asked the owner questions. Then he hung up. "He says he's coming down with the key so we can try it out."

"Thanks for doing this," Bea said. "I don't know anything about boats, really. It helps to have you here, since you're the expert."

"Happy to help. It's fun for me. I never thought I'd see the day when my big-city sister would move back to Coral Island and buy a run-around. But here we are."

She slapped his arm playfully. "I'm still the same girl deep down that I always was."

"Some things don't change, I suppose." He pretended to duck away from her swatting hand. "Like your propensity for violence."

She rolled her eyes. "And your tendency to exaggerate."

The owner of the boat showed up within a few minutes and handed them the key. Bradford started the boat while Bea climbed on board. She donned a life jacket, which the owner insisted on for both of them, then sat down and held on as Brad guided the boat out of the marina and accelerated out to sea.

She held on to her hat and narrowed her eyes against the blast of wind in her face. It felt good to be out on the water and to forget about her worries for a few minutes. She was more fearful about Harry's health than she let on to anyone else. He wasn't the type of boy to lie about in bed most of the day. He was skinnier and paler than usual as well, and his appetite was nothing like it'd been when they lived together in Sydney. She hoped it wasn't anything serious. Being out on the ocean gave her a chance to push those thoughts aside and focus on the task at hand — she was buying a boat of her very own. The idea gave her a little thrill.

Brad slowed the boat as they neared the point where their father's house sat, in stoic silence, atop a steep cliff. He glanced up at the house, then let the boat drift slowly around the point.

"What do you think?" he asked, facing her with one hand on the steering wheel.

"I like it. It's exactly what I'm looking for. But I suppose it would be silly to buy the first thing we look at."

"Not necessarily," he said. "If it's what you're looking for and the price is right, you should jump on it. I doubt there are many like it available on Coral Island, so we'd have to go to the mainland to look further."

"That's true. If the engine checks out, I think I should go for it."

"I do too. Come on—have a turn at driving just to be sure."

She shifted into place behind the steering wheel and steadied her hand on the thrust. Excitement sent a tingle down her spine. She pushed down on the accelerator, and the boat dove forwards, rising up at the same time and causing her to lose her balance. She hadn't expected it to be quite so responsive. She stumbled into her brother, who caught her before tripping over his own feet and tumbling backwards over the edge of the boat into the water. Before Bea could help it, she'd followed him and plunged backwards, headfirst into the ocean. The water was cold and stole her breath from her lungs as she worked to right herself.

When her head popped through the water's surface, the boat had come to a stop and was idling nearby. There was no sign of Brad.

She coughed and spluttered, then yelled, "Brad! Brad! Where are you?"

Panic lit up her senses as adrenaline spiked through her

veins. Where could he be? He fell in the ocean only a moment before she did.

Just then, she saw a tall black form slide into the boat with a grunt. She exhaled with relief. He sat up panting, then waved and drove the boat back to where she floated. He helped her up.

"I wasn't expecting that," he said. "I don't know what happened, but I got my foot caught on something, so when you ran into me, I toppled out." He kicked at a rope coiled on the bottom of the boat. "It must've been this."

"I'm so sorry," Bea said between gasping breaths. "I've spent so much time on boats, but this one moved faster than I'm used to."

"It's got a more powerful motor than the ones you've putted around the island in," he said with a laugh. "Just as well the owner made you wear that life jacket. You should probably always put one on, given your lack of coordination."

"Thanks a lot," Bea said dryly. Although he wasn't wrong. That would be the top of her list — buying life jackets for herself and any passengers.

"At least the boat has a kill switch, so it stopped immediately."

"Thank goodness."

By now, they'd idled around the end of the point and the boat had turned so it was facing the cliffs around the bend from where their father's house stood. If they kept going with the tide, they'd end up looking directly at Bea's cottage before long. But they had to get back to the marina, or the owner of the boat would think they'd stolen it.

She looked at the cliff face, studying the curve of the blackened rocks and the brown of the clay segments. "It's beautiful, isn't it?"

Bradford was busy coiling the rope to move it elsewhere. "Huh? Oh, yeah. I love it here. I often dive nearby."

"What's that cave there, in the cliff face? Have you ever seen it before?" It was low against the rocks, a dark cavern pressed into the side of the hill.

He squinted. "No, I don't think I've seen it. The tide is usually high when I come out here. But I haven't paid too much attention. I don't like to get close to the shore—the the tide can pull you in against those rocks so fast. I tend to moor my boat further out when I'm diving."

"I might take a walk later and see if I can find it."

"You won't see it once the tide rises."

She sat shivering, hugging herself as Bradford drove them back to the marina. The wind was cold now that she was wet, and they hadn't brought towels to dry themselves with. Her joggers were sodden, along with her jeans and shirt. Her hair dripped cold water down her spine, and she'd lost her hat in the ocean.

A few moments later, she sought refuge beside Bradford. The air didn't buffet her as wildly when she sheltered behind the centre console with her brother.

"Did I tell you I'm looking into Mary Brown's murder?" she shouted over the noise of the boat and the rush of wind.

He shook his head.

"Do you remember those photos I found at the cottage?"

A nod.

"They're linked somehow to the murder."

"Are you sure?"

"Not exactly. But Penny's family are in the photos, along with some other people like Buck and June Clements."

"So, who's the murderer, Agatha?" he asked, eyes twinkling.

She hesitated. The truth was, she had her suspicions, but she didn't have proof. "I don't know for sure. But I have someone in mind. I'll tell you when I've got evidence to back up my hunch."

"Okay, sounds good. But can I ask you to do something for me?"

She leaned against the side of the boat. "Sure. What is it?"

"Be careful."

Twelve

AS THE FERRY pulled away from the island, a lump rose in Penny's throat. She waved wildly one last time, even though she knew Rowan couldn't see her. He was safely ensconced in his vehicle somewhere on the ferry, out of sight.

It was early morning, and the sun shone brightly after a night of light rainfall and a brief thunderstorm. The world looked as though it'd been washed clean, and the ocean was calm and blue. As Penny's arm dropped back to her side, the sunlight caught on her engagement ring, making it sparkle and glint. She studied it a moment, turning it side to side so the blue stone caught the light.

She'd never been one for jewellery, but she had to admit, she'd fallen in love with this ring. It was beautiful, and the single nicest piece she'd ever owned in her life. She was constantly panicked it would fall off in the mud and be lost forever. Grateful it was a firm fit, she looked it over one more time before climbing into her car for the drive home.

Rowan had left for Israel. He had a story to cover. And as much as she hated that he had to go, she knew he'd come back now that she had her ring. Before he proposed, she'd worried he might return to his life on the road and forget all about her. She hadn't been sure how much his feelings mirrored hers. Especially after he'd said they weren't serious.

It didn't matter now, though. They were getting married, and she couldn't be happier about it, even if she did feel a cloying sense of panic every now and then at the thought of it. That was just nerves. Everyone experienced nerves before they were married. Didn't they?

The one thing that bothered her was the family connection between them. According to Rowan and his mother, June, his father was a fisherman who'd never returned to the island. But the man who'd raised him was Buck Clements — who she now knew was her own biological father. She hadn't told Rowan any of this yet, since she wasn't sure how to raise the subject.

She didn't want to push Rowan, but if Buck Clements was her father, then there was a slight chance they were related. What if Buck was Rowan's father, not just his stepdad? But why would June lie about something like that? No, that didn't make sense. Still, it niggled at her.

Even if there was no blood relationship, there was a strange family connection that was more than a coincidence. His stepfather had taken advantage of her mother when she was still a teen. That wasn't Rowan's fault, but the two of them hadn't spoken about it since she discovered the truth. She knew she should tell him, but how?

How did she break the news to her fiancé that his stepfather, a man he'd only recently forgiven and reconnected with, had a relationship with her mother? How could she reveal the truth of her parenthood? It would devastate him. He deserved to know the truth, but she hated to break his heart. Her own was hurting enough for the both of them. It was a hard truth to face—her father was a predator, and her mother, his victim. What else was he hiding?

She pulled out of the parking lot with a weight pressing against her chest, her throat tight. It was too much for her to process, let alone talk about. She needed more time.

Her phone rang—it was the sanctuary. They'd received a call about an owl in distress over at Amity Point. She said she'd take a look and turned at the next intersection in that direction. Amity Point was where Buck Clements lived. She could check out the owl and visit him while she was there. Maybe he'd have some answers to the questions that plagued her thoughts.

She needed a degree of resolution before she could happily marry the man of her dreams. If she didn't learn the truth soon, she might chicken out of the wedding entirely, and that would be unfair to Rowan and herself. She'd spent decades wishing and hoping she might someday find a loving, kind, fun man to share her life with. She didn't want to ruin it now with a decades-old secret.

* * *

The bird they'd received the call about turned out to be a tawny frogmouth, not an owl, although the creature looked remarkably owllike with its large eyes, oversized head and tawny feathers. It had a broken wing and was nestled in the corner of an elderly lady's back porch, unwilling to move on. She'd given it a bowl of water and Penny secured it in a travel cage to take back to the animal refuge with her, since it would starve to death if left to its own devices while the wing healed.

"Do you know how it ended up on your porch?" she asked as she carefully guided the creature into the cage, wings held in place to keep it from flapping.

The woman pressed a finger to her lips. "Maybe a cat chased it up here, I really couldn't say."

"It doesn't seem to be missing any feathers, which would

indicate an altercation with a cat," Penny said as she shut the door on the cage and lifted it in one hand. "Usually a broken wing would result from a run-in with a car."

"It's possible," the woman replied, "then I guess it climbed my stairs. I wasn't home last night — out playing MahJong with my friends at the local community centre."

"That sounds like fun," Penny replied.

"Oh, we love it. It's a regular game with the same people every week. We have teams of four at each table. And there's often live music as well. Buck was on the guitar last night, and he's quite the talent." The woman waved her hands about as she spoke, her blue eyes obscured behind thick spectacles.

"Buck Clements?" Penny asked, her interest piqued.

"That's right. Do you know him?"

"I've met him. He's a guitarist?"

"Very musically gifted. I think he said he was a studio guitarist in Nashville in his younger days."

"Really?" Penny's brow furrowed. There was so much she didn't know about the man. Rowan had never mentioned his affiliation with Nashville. But the truth was, Rowan had barely spoken of his step father in all the time she'd known him, so the oversight wasn't surprising.

As she drove away with the bird safely ensconced in the back of her vehicle, Penny's thoughts wandered. Who was this man? How had she spent a lifetime on this small island without ever running into him or hearing about him? Why were the reports about him now so conflicted? Was he a monster or a gifted musician? A recluse or a friendly neighbour who attended weekly MahJong games? An angry, abusive husband or a misunderstood stepfather? A predator or a loving family man?

The neighbourhood was green and lush after several weeks of on-and-off rain. Trees with creeping vines hanging from their branches lined the small lane where Buck lived. The road was dark with dappled sunlight leaving a golden leaf-shaped pattern on the tarmac. Her vehicle crept along the road as her heart hammered against her ribcage. This was it, there was no turning back. Once she confronted the man with what she knew, there was no way to pretend she didn't know he was her father. No way to avoid the awkward truth about her existence. No way to forget what he'd done. Was it too late for him to be held accountable?

She didn't know much about the law. The police hadn't thought charges were warranted at the time. Or maybe they didn't know all the facts. Regardless, her goal was to discover the truth and to connect with the man she'd spent her entire life wondering about. She'd run through so many scenarios in her head as a child where she might accidentally come across her father, and he'd be so happy to see her, so proud of her that even the memory of those imaginings brought a tear to her eye.

She dashed the tears away with the back of her hand and climbed out of the vehicle, then fetched the animal carrier from the back and stood at the end of Buck's driveway steeling her nerves. His house was homely and warm. Painted white with grey trim, it was nestled in a delightfully arranged and impeccably maintained cottage garden. A large avocado tree with sprawling branches occupied most of the front yard, and several pieces of fruit lay dotted across the ground below, green skin turned black in places and several with chunks missing.

With a deep breath, she strode down the drive and knocked on the door. It sprang open beneath her knuckles, and she heard the sound of music playing in another room. She knocked again, this time louder, as she peered around the door, attempting to get a look inside.

The house hadn't changed since the last time she visited only a few months earlier with her friends and Rowan. But her perspective was different. Last time she'd been there was as a curious outsider. This time, she had a new interest in learning more about this man. It was still difficult for her to say the word "father," but she tried it out now inside her head. Father. He was her father. She startled when he poked his head around the doorframe with a frown.

His moustache twitched. "Howdy. I've met you before, haven't I?"

"Yes, that's right, Mr Clements. I'm Penny St James. We met when I visited a while ago with Rowan and some of my friends."

"Yes, that's right. Come on in, Miss St James. I'm sorry, I'm covered in dirt and sweat. I've been out in the garden, and the humidity is a drag today."

"It's unusually warm for winter, that's for sure," she admitted, following him into the kitchen.

"What can I do for you, young lady?" he asked, washing his hands in the sink.

She cleared her throat. "I'd hoped I might talk to you about something."

"Of course, take a seat. Would you like a cup of coffee? I was about to make one for myself."

He brewed coffee for them both using a small espresso machine on his bench. As he made the coffee, he chattered on about his garden, what grew best, the plants he was struggling with, and the things that thrived without any help. Penny couldn't help thinking she found a resemblance between his love of gardening and her passion for animals. His attention to detail as he described the various lengths he'd gone to in order to get his blueberry bush to produce fruit was remarkably like her own efforts to construct the perfect habitat for the residents of her animal shelter.

Did she have his nose? What colour had his hair been before it became the white-grey colour it was now? So many questions without answers. She wanted to discover it all. But she was angry, too. It bubbled beneath the surface, though she did her best to quash it. How could he have done the things he did? Why did he treat her mother that way? She couldn't really believe he was responsible for her grandmother's murder, could she? This man in front of her, so enamoured with his plants, so committed to gardening, as he poured espresso into matching china cups and set one in front of her. He appeared so harmless, friendly and even likeable. She couldn't imagine him harming anyone.

Before long, they'd covered a number of subjects, and still her heart was in her throat, waiting for the right moment to change the topic of conversation. He brought out an apple crumb cake and cut her a slice. It melted in her mouth, and she wished she could take another slice home with her.

Finally, there was a lull in the conversation, and she dove into the subject she'd wanted to address since the moment she arrived.

"The reason I came today... I discovered something. My mother, Ruby St James, told me that you're my biological father." There was no point warming up to the subject. She had to get it out before she burst.

His smile faded, and he stood to his feet, clearing away her empty coffee cup. "That can't be right. I never had children of my own. Only a stepson."

She followed him. "Do you remember Ruby? You knew her when she was young, I believe. Her name was Ruby Brown back then. She was Mary's daughter."

He faced her, lips puckered in thought. "Let's see now. Ruby... Oh, yeah, I recall a girl with that name. She was a friend of my wife, June, for a while there."

"That's right. She's my mother."

"Look, I don't know what she told you or why, but she's not my type. Besides that, I was married when I knew her."

"Not the whole time," Penny replied, her confidence

fading. "Before she got pregnant, you were single. The two of you had an affair. She told me everything. I'd hoped you might be willing to talk about it now, since so much time has passed. I'm not here to blame you for anything. I only want to get to know you."

He ran fingers through his grey hair so that it looked messy, and he seemed older than he had a few moments earlier. She noticed for the first time the bags beneath his red-rimmed eyes. "I'm telling you, it isn't possible. Now, if you could give me some space, I'm feeling mighty tired after several hours in the garden, and I'd really like to lie down."

He ushered her towards the front door.

"Of course, but do you mind if I use the bathroom before I go? I'm busting, and I still have to get this bird back to the refuge." She picked up the animal carrier, and the bird peered out through large yellow eyes.

"Fine, fine. It's through here."

She went into the bathroom and stood staring into the small mirror above the sink for several long moments. Did she look like him? Was he really her father? Her resolve had begun to waver in the face of his denial. Perhaps her mother was wrong. Although it wasn't something a sixteen-year-old would really lie about. No, he had to be her father. There was no other possible explanation for her existence.

She opened the medicine cabinet behind the mirror and looked through the items on the shelves. The standard toiletries were there, along with a few bottles of medicine. There was also a comb containing several strands of grey hair. She grabbed the hairs off the comb and shoved them into a small resealable baggie she had in her pocket that'd contained a brownie earlier but now held only crumbs. Then she washed her hands and left.

As she drove away, her pulse raced. She shouldn't have done it, but she had to know the truth. Was Buck her father?

If she could run a DNA test on his hair, maybe she could prove their connection. It was worth a try.

* * *

Back at the beach house, Penny took a shower to wash off the mud and filth of a day traipsing around the countryside to rescue injured animals and managing the wildlife refuge. There was mud in places she hadn't expected, along with the pungent odour a nervous possum had left on her shorts.

After the shower, she felt refreshed. She padded to the kitchen in a sundress to pour herself a glass of cucumber water — her latest addiction. She sipped it while studying the picture frames she'd purchased from an antique store to hold the photographs Beatrice had given her of her family. The photos that'd been hidden for fifty years in Bea's cottage.

She fetched the printed photographs from the desk in her office and slipped them into the frames. Then she hung them in the hallway. After taking a few steps back, she tipped her head from side to side to examine the effect. Happy with the result, she took another sip of water. It felt good to have photographs of her family from so long ago hanging in her house.

Thirteen

THE VISIT to the doctor's office with Harry was brief but worrying for Beatrice. The doctor was more concerned she'd thought he would be, and Harry appeared more peaked than he had earlier. She was feeling anxious. What if it was something serious? She'd never considered that either of her children might leave this earth before her. She wasn't sure she could face something like that. Her heart clattered against her ribcage. No, she was supposed to go before them. It wouldn't be right.

She patted his arm as they sat in the chair outside the clinic waiting for his blood to be drawn. "It's going to be okay."

Her intention was to calm his worries, but instead she exacerbated her own. She'd always been the one to help him feel better, to tell him things weren't as bad as he thought. But this time, she wasn't convinced of the truth of her own words. It might not be okay.

"I know, Mum. I'm sure it's the flu or something."

"Although it's lasted a little longer than it should, really."

"And I feel so bad. I haven't wanted to worry you, but there's this horrible feeling inside me."

"What kind of feeling?" She swivelled in her chair to study him, brow furrowed.

"Like I'm suffocating. Not really—I'm not sure how to describe it. But I don't feel as though I'm really here or something. Like I'm in a fog."

She shook her head. This wasn't good. "Well, we're here to find out what's going on, so let's not jump to any conclusions yet. We'll make ourselves anxious without reason."

"Thanks, Mum. I'm glad you're here."

The woman taking blood came outside the small room to collect Harry. Beatrice remained behind in the waiting room. He emerged a few minutes later with a small Band-Aid on his arm.

"Let's go," he said.

They drove back to the cottage in silence. Harry stared out the window. Bea glanced worriedly at him every few minutes. If she could only get him to eat, surely he'd begin to feel better soon.

"We'll see what the doctor says in a few days. Until then, let's just forget about all this. Try to enjoy our last few days of holidays together."

"I don't think I should go back to Sydney," Harry said softly.

"Oh." Bea bit down on her lip. She hadn't realised he was so unwell until very recently. She was a horrible mother not to have noticed just how bad things had gotten. Guilt washed over her.

"I'm not up to it. I don't know what's wrong, but I can't go back to uni feeling like this. I won't be able to get anything done. Is it okay if I just stay here at the cottage with you? I'll postpone my degree for a semester. I'm sure it'll be fine."

"Of course it's okay," she assured him. "You take all the time you need. We can call the university tomorrow."

When they reached the cottage, Bea marvelled at the way

the climbing vine she'd planted next to the structure had managed to wind its way halfway up the trellis already. There were no flowers this time of year, but when spring began in a few weeks' time, there would be an abundance of pink flowers all over it. She was excited about the garden's growth. The cottage looked quaint and welcoming, unlike the run-down wreck it'd been only a short time ago before her renovations.

Dani was waiting for them in the kitchen. She stirred a pot of chilli with one hand, her gaze flitting to find Bea's the moment she walked through the door. Her blonde hair was pulled high into a very short ponytail. Her brown eyes were wide.

"So? What did the doctor say?"

"Nothing yet. He did a blood test, so we'll find out the results in a few days."

"Okay." Dani's nostrils flared.

Bea knew how worried her daughter was, although she hadn't said much about it. But the two siblings loved each other deeply, and Dani had always taken on a motherly role with her younger brother, especially when he was hurt or in trouble.

Harry sat down at the table, shoulders slouched. Bea hurried to set the table for an early dinner so Harry could eat and go to bed. The sound of Aidan's truck pulling up outside the cottage sent her scurrying to open the door. She kissed him on the lips and leaned against his firm chest as he hugged her close.

"It's good to see you. That smells delicious."

Grace was with him. She didn't wait to be invited, instead bounding inside with a wide grin to greet Dani and Harry. Bea enjoyed witnessing her growing confidence. She was glad Grace felt so at home with them. It was a huge relief to Aidan, she knew. He so badly wanted his daughter to feel as though she belonged with him on the island, and Bea was grateful for anything she and her family could do to help him with that aim.

"How's school going?" she asked Grace as they all sat down to eat.

"Fine, I guess."

"What do you plan on doing while you're staying with your dad?"

Her nose wrinkled. "He says he's going to teach me to bait a hook. But I don't know… Sounds kind of gross."

Dani laughed. "You'll get the hang of it in no time. It's really not that bad. Gutting the fish, though… That's an entirely different matter. I still can't do it. I make Mum or Uncle Brad do it for me."

"That's true, she does," Bea agreed. "Maybe Dani can go with you this time."

As the conversation continued, she did her best to focus on things that might reduce her anxiety levels. The homely feel of the cottage, the family photos hanging on the walls. The white Hamptons-style furniture she'd picked out that gave the entire place a romantic beachy feel. The sound of the waves shushing in the distance. The glow of pink and orange through the kitchen window as the sun set over the island. Gradually, her heart rate slowed and her breathing returned to normal.

I can't control everything.

It was a mantra a counsellor had once taught her years ago when she'd first struggled to overcome chronic anxiety after Dani was born.

I can't control the world. I can only control myself.

She ran through the mantra again, reminding herself to let go of the fear that sometimes returned to cripple her. She'd managed to keep it at bay for decades until her recent divorce had brought it all tumbling back.

"You okay, Mum?" Dani asked, concern etched across her

delicate features. The small freckles on her nose stood out more than usual after a day in the sun.

"Fine," she replied. "I'm thinking about Harry. But no doubt he's going to be okay."

"I'm worried too," Dani admitted, glancing at her brother. "How do you feel, Harry?"

Harry looked up from the bowl where he'd been pushing chilli around with a spoon. "Huh?"

"Do you feel unwell?" Bea asked.

"Tired, a little foggy. Not really hungry."

"Try to eat something," she urged.

"And how about you?" Aidan asked, turning his attention to Dani. "Tell us all about university."

Dani reluctantly pulled her eyes away from her brother's pale face. "Um... It's good. I'm loving interior design. Much better than social work — it suits me better, anyway. I'm more creative than I realised, I guess."

"You're very creative," Bea agreed.

"Thanks, Mum. But you have to say that."

"No, it's true," Grace added, her cheeks pink. "I love the art you did for the walls." She pointed to the pieces that hung in the living room. They could see them quite well from the dining table since the cottage was so cosy.

"I'm glad you like it. It makes me happy. So, that's something I hadn't realised about myself until recently. And I've met someone, too."

Bea's mouth fell open. She shut it again quickly. "Really?"

"Yes. His name is Damien, and he's at university with me. Architecture department."

"Is it serious?" Aidan asked before slipping a giant spoonful of chilli into his mouth.

"We're not dating or anything, just friends. But I like him. He's nice—funny, too."

Bea broke crackers into pieces, slowly adding them to her bowl. "Funny is code for cute."

Dani rolled her eyes. "No, it's not. He really is funny. And he wants to come to Coral Island with me in the summer holidays."

Bea arched an eyebrow. "Oh..."

"It's okay, Mum. I promise."

"Well, let's talk about it closer to the time. Okay?" It was highly possible Dani would've moved on to someone else by then. But if they were still "friends", perhaps Damien could stay with Dad up on the hill. He certainly wouldn't be staying in the cottage — there was barely enough room for the three of them.

This was a first for her — Dani had never had a serious boyfriend in high school, and Harry hadn't dated a girl ever, as far as she knew. She'd have to put some thought into how to handle the situation.

Fourteen

BLUE SHOAL WAS at its best in the evenings when the sun had dipped towards the horizon and the sky became a cacophony of colours that bathed the world in purple, pink and orange hues with golden fingers reaching over the jewelled ocean.

As Taya jogged around the marina, she soaked it all in — the beauty of the place she'd called home for most of her life. She was born on the mainland, but had grown up in Blue Shoal. She'd moved away for a short while to attend university, but when she married Todd Futcher, they'd moved back to Blue Shoal to open the inn. And she'd stayed there ever since.

There was something about the loss of her lover, best friend and confidante in this place that kept her anchored to it. Could she ever let go of the inn and move on with her life if it meant finally letting go of Todd?

The grief she'd been through when he died was something she never wanted to face again. Her responsibility, the fact that she'd had to keep putting one foot in front of the other to keep the inn running, was the thing that'd given her the strength to continue living. That and their daughter, who'd been so young at the time that she barely understood what was going on.

But now Camden was a woman. She didn't live on the island. Soon she'd be a professionally trained chef, and it wasn't likely she'd move back to Blue Shoal. At least, not in the short term. She enjoyed her life in Cairns, and Taya was happy for her. She wanted nothing more than for her daughter to be fulfilled and safe, no matter where she lived. But Taya had to admit that she was lonely. The inn was shut for renovations. Her daughter was busy living her life on the mainland. And Taya found herself with more time on her hands than she'd had in her entire adult life.

The renovations were costing her more than she'd originally set aside. She'd taken out another line of credit from the bank, but that would be gone soon as well. Every time they did anything, more expense was incurred. When they replaced the roof and found water damage, it sparked structural work, which revealed termite damage, requiring more structural work. New lighting for each room had uncovered the need for a complete electrical update. Her electrician had also told her the law required her to replace every single smoke detector with new, higher-tech equipment. And on and on.

It was like pulling on the end of a ball of yarn—the more she pulled, the faster it unravelled until her bank account had been cleaned out and she was wondering if she'd even be able to afford to reopen the place. If she did reopen, would people come? There was no way for her to know without doing it, but how would she pay the staff or buy the supplies she needed? In the end, the renovation had been a disastrous idea, but if she didn't do it, the inn would've had to close anyway.

She'd taken to running every afternoon. In the mornings, she swam laps in the bay. During the day, she managed the renovation project and bugged Penny, Evie and Beatrice with unannounced drop-ins, requests for coffee, and had even raised the idea of joining Evie's book club. But so far, they'd all been very patient with her, and she was more appreciative than she'd let on. They seemed to sense her desperation, but were too kind to mention it.

Still, she was aware that she needed something more in her life, something to give her a sense of purpose. That'd always been the inn, or her daughter, before now. And the change in circumstances drew light to the fact that she'd kept herself busy in order not to face the truth — she was treading water and had no idea what she wanted to do with her life.

The pounding of her feet on the pavement resounded like a song and she studied the path ahead, her thoughts whirling. She glanced up and saw a man crouching at the end of the path where it met the street. He reached out a hand towards a bush, and she slowed her pace, frowning.

What was going on?

The man was tall and slender, dressed in shorts and a T-shirt. His dark brown hair was pushed back away from a tanned face, and he was intently fixated upon something or someone in that bush. As she drew closer, she reduced her speed until she was walking. It was then she recognised him.

"Hi, Andrew," she said.

He looked up, startled at the sound of his name. "Taya — I'm glad you're here. Do you know anything about dogs?"

His soft, lilting Indian accent was stronger today than it had been the previous times she'd spoken with him. He looked younger too, in shorts and a T-shirt. His face seemed to have aged backwards, and her heart skipped a beat as she drew closer.

"Dogs? Um, no, not really. What are you doing?"

"There's a dog huddled here in this shrub. It looks in need of some medical attention, but I can't get it to come to me."

Taya peered beneath the shrubbery and saw a small black

dog with matted hair. It was leaning back on its haunches, the whites of its eyes showing.

She held out a hand and called in a soft voice, "Come on, come here." The dog moved forwards slowly and went to her, sniffing her fingers carefully before allowing her to pat it.

"How did you do that?" Andrew straightened, his brow furrowed.

"I don't know, really. I've never had a dog, but they seem to like me anyway."

"They can tell you have a good heart."

"I don't know if that's true."

"Look, I was going to take the dog to the vet to get checked out before they close. I only have about fifteen minutes—I called them earlier to find out. Do you think you could help me? I'm not sure it'll get into my car without you."

She glanced around the marina. There was nowhere in particular she had to be. "But what if you're a serial killer? My parents always taught me not to get into a car with a stranger."

He laughed. "That's a good point. I suppose you could sit in the back with the dog for protection. It doesn't seem to like me much."

"Does that mean you don't have a good heart?"

He feigned hurt, clutching at his chest. "Ugh, that was harsh."

She laughed. He was cute when he flirted.

His brown eyes flashed. "Come on. I'll buy you dinner as payment for your service as a dog whisperer."

Was it a date? Or was he being friendly? She couldn't tell. But whatever his offer meant, it was better than spending her evening in front of the television eating day-old salad with a can of tuna on top.

"That sounds nice. Okay, let's go." She took a gentle hold of the dog's collar and led it to his car. It didn't resist and hopped easily into the back seat. She sat with it, and it cradled

THE BLUE SHOAL INN

its head on her lap as Andrew drove them to the vet. His car was immaculately clean with leather seats and not a single piece of rubbish. She was impressed. Her vehicle was generally mud splattered from four-wheel driving, although the inside was usually spotless. She liked to keep things tidy. Her friends made fun of her—called her OCD.

They talked easily on the drive. She wondered how she'd managed to get him so wrong in the short time she'd known him. Out of his business attire, he was much more easy-going, relaxed and friendly than she'd expected him to be. Perhaps she'd misjudged him entirely.

When the vet returned the dog to them, the animal seemed more at ease. Its tongue hung out of its mouth as it panted, and the vet had attached a rope to its collar. The vet was a short woman with blonde hair and kind green eyes.

"This little girl is in good health," the vet said. "She needs a bath and a flea treatment. Here's a bag with the medicine in it. But there's no ID number or chip, so we have no way of knowing who she belongs to. Someone has fed her until recently, though, so perhaps you should advertise. Anyway, she'll need a place to stay tonight."

The woman eyed Andrew and Taya one at a time. Andrew spoke up first. "Oh, she can stay at my place. I have plenty of room."

"Great. You'll need food and shampoo. There's a pet shop next door."

Andrew paid the vet, and they hurried next door for supplies before the shop closed. They were the last customers, and the shop attendant shut and locked the door behind them as they stepped outside with their purchases.

"Well, that was close. I'm glad it all worked out. I suppose we'll have to put up fliers or something to see if her owner is looking for her."

"I'll do that tomorrow," Andrew said. "Thanks for your help."

"You're welcome."

"I promised you dinner," he said.

"Yes, but you don't have to follow through. I'm sure you're tired..." She was giving him an out, but dreaded the thought of going home to her empty house alone.

He put the dog into his car, then opened the passenger door for her. "Come on, I'll order us a pizza. I think I have some wine at home. It's not much, but I'd really like to do this as a thank you. If it wasn't for you, I'd still be sitting next to the footpath trying to coax the dog out from under the bush."

"I'm glad I could help."

"So, pizza?"

"Okay. That would be nice."

He drove her back to his place. She was surprised by how warm and homely it was, a nineteen-sixties timber home set on stilts at the top of a low, sloping hill. She walked inside and gasped — the entire back wall was made of concertina glass doors with a view over the dark ocean. Andrew carried the dog inside and set her down. She looked around, then trotted off to investigate the place.

"It's beautiful!" Taya said.

He set his keys in a bowl on a narrow timber table. "It's the main reason I bought this place. I fell in love with that view. The house isn't very big, but I don't need much space since it's only me living here. And I can sit anywhere in the living area or on the deck outside and look at that." He waved a hand in the direction of the doors.

"I would've done the same thing," she said.

She wandered over to the windows while Andrew ordered pizza. He finished up the order and emerged from the all-white kitchen with two glasses of red wine.

"I hope you like wine."

She took the offered glass. "Thank you. I love it. Not sure it's exactly what I need after a run..."

"Of course, I'll get you some water. I should've thought of that."

He opened the glass sliding door, and she stepped outside, leaning against the railing. He returned shortly with her water, and she downed it in two long gulps.

"That's better."

"You enjoy running?" he asked, folding his long frame into a white wicker chair.

She sat opposite him. "I do. It helps me with anxiety."

"I'm sure the renovation is stressful," he said. "I've done a few of those myself, and it can sometimes feel as though everything is going wrong."

"Yes! That's exactly it," she replied. "I keep hoping it will come together smoothly, but something disastrous always happens to ruin my plans."

The dog walked out to join them and nosed Taya's leg. She laughed. "What a cutie."

"I'll get her something to eat," Andrew said, rising. "And I'm sure she's thirsty."

"What will you call her? I mean, until you find her owner?" she asked, following him inside.

"I don't know. Any suggestions?"

"We had a dog called Maisy once. How about Daisy?"

"Daisy? I like it. Let's call her Daisy. I'm sure we'll locate her owner quickly—it's not a very big community. I bet she misses home."

She leaned against the kitchen counter while he poured the newly purchased dog food into a shiny silver bowl.

"I know a little something about missing home," he continued.

"You're homesick?" she asked.

"I worked for your father in the Cairns office for a number

of years before I moved here. And prior to that, I lived in Chennai, India, with my family. I grew up there and I miss it every day."

"Is your family still there?"

"Yes, I haven't visited them in many years. We didn't see eye to eye about a few things."

She didn't want to pry, but was curious what could've happened to keep him away from his family. She'd had plenty of disagreements over the years with her own parents, but couldn't imagine going years without seeing them. "Oh, I'm sorry to hear that."

"When my wife was killed by extremists outside her mosque, my family refused to condemn them. I asked my father to speak out, to say it was wrong. He has a lot of influence in our community, but he wouldn't do it. After that, I left and never returned. It was ten years ago."

Taya didn't know what to say. She'd never experienced anything remotely like what he was referring to, and her heart ached for him. "I'm so sorry, Andrew. Losing her must've been absolutely devastating for you. And your family wouldn't stand up for her? I can't imagine how that must've felt."

"Thank you. I appreciate it. I don't like to talk about it—I'm not sure why I'm bringing it up now. Only . . . I suppose I feel safe around you." His brown eyes crinkled at the edges.

The doorbell rang, and he hurried to answer it. He returned with two hot pizzas and set them on the small table outside. They sat together and ate, talking and laughing together. Taya felt much more comfortable around him now than she had before. He'd opened up and shared a piece of his past, something he didn't tell everyone. His revelation had pried open her heart a little, and she felt the tenderness it exposed. He could hurt her heart—she knew that, but she could hurt him too, and he'd been willing to trust her with his most painful secret.

It seemed she'd misjudged him. She'd taken in his polished, suave appearance and assumed he was as slick as his suits and Italian loafers. But beneath his fashionable clothing and perfectly sculpted athletic physique was a man whose heart had been broken and whose family had abandoned him when he needed them most.

She could no longer blame him for the fate of her inn. It was something she'd have to deal with on her own. And with money sifting through her bank account like sand, she'd have to make a decision sooner than she'd anticipated.

Fifteen

BEATRICE LEFT the doctor's office with Harry, his shoulders hunched. He climbed into the car in silence, then sighed and stared out the window as she pulled out of the car park.

"You okay?" she asked.

He grunted. "Lyme disease? I don't really even know what that means. I wanted to ask questions, but I was in shock. When would I have gotten a tick bite?"

"I don't know," Beatrice admitted. She racked her brain to remember the last time he'd gone hiking or camping. Anything that might've put him in the path of a wayward tick. But she couldn't think of it. Maybe it would come to her later —she could get out her diary and trace back through it looking for clues. Sometimes it was helpful that she kept track of most of the things that happened in her life in an ongoing series of journals. Most of the time, though, she wondered if it was a complete waste — who would ever read it? "Can you recall anything?"

He slapped his forehead. "I went bushwalking with a group from uni a few months ago. That must be it. There was a tick—I completely forgot about it. I didn't think anything of it."

Beatrice inhaled a slow breath. Whatever happened, they'd deal with it together. At least now they knew what they were facing.

"I thought it was the flu," he said.

She'd feared something worse, so her concern was tinged with relief. But she couldn't admit that to him. "I'm glad we know. Now we can decide what to do about it."

He flicked through the pamphlet the doctor had given them. "I'm so tired. I'm glad you called the university to postpone my studies. I couldn't focus feeling the way I do."

"It's for the best that you stay here with me for as long as you need."

"Thanks, Mum," he whispered, pushing the hair out of his eyes with one hand. For a moment, he looked so young, like her little boy again. His brown eyes were full of worry, but she could tell he was doing his best not to show it.

"Of course, honey. I'll take care of you. You can relax, spend time in the sun, get some rest." One thing she hadn't figured out yet was what she'd do with the café. If she was taking care of Harry, how could she run her new business at the same time?

She pulled into the driveway in front of her father's house, and he opened the door to greet them.

"I wasn't expecting the two of you," he said. "Come in. I'll brew some tea."

They sat in the kitchen, with Harry and Bea on barstools at the long bench while Dad boiled the kettle and spooned leaves into the teapot. She explained what they'd learned at the doctor's office, and Dad listened with a frown.

"Harry can stay here during the day," he said suddenly. "I know you're busy with work. I'm here most of the time. We can spend that time together, or he can sleep in the guest room."

"That would definitely help me feel a lot better about things," Bea admitted, noticing a ball of tightness in her chest began to loosen at his words.

"Thanks, Pa."

Dad ruffled Harry's hair with one hand as he passed him a cup of tea. "Anytime, kiddo."

"I'll drink my tea, but then I have to go," Bea said. "Dani is traveling back to Sydney at lunchtime, and I've got to get back to the café and make sure they haven't burned the place to the ground."

Dad chuckled. "Sounds like a busy day. Make sure you stop here so I can give Dani a goodbye kiss."

"Will do." She hurriedly downed the rest of her tea, then rushed out to her car.

She found Dani in her bedroom, bag almost packed and a look of frustration on her face.

"Why doesn't it all fit?" Dani asked. "I haven't added anything. It's the same amount of stuff I brought with me, and it fit last time. But I can't manage to get it all back into my suitcase."

Bea hugged her from behind. Dani swivelled to kiss her cheek.

"I'm gonna miss you, sweetheart."

"Me too," Dani said. "I'll miss you even more if you pack my bag for me."

Bea grunted. "I'm glad you still need me for some things. By the way, we found out your brother has Lyme disease." Bea unloaded the clothes from Dani's bag and began folding them neatly.

"What's that?" Dani asked.

"It's from a tick bite."

"Really? Wow, Harry's not exactly the outdoors-y type."

"No, he's not. But the important thing is, he's going to be okay."

* * *

By the time she'd dropped Dani at the ferry terminal and waved her off, Bea's stress levels had risen substantially. She hated leaving the café on a day when there wasn't enough casual staff to manage, and one of the girls who covered for her on the weekends was busy during the week and unable to fill in for her.

She rushed into the cafe expecting trouble but the place was quiet. Everything looked in order. The few customers who were there had cups of coffee and pieces of cake on the small tables in front of them. She sighed with relief that all seemed in order and proceeded at a more sedate pace to the kitchen to tie her apron in place.

Candace, a nineteen-year-old with short brown hair that fell in a blunt fringe across her eyes, stepped out from behind the counter to greet Bea. She rarely smiled, but her eyes were large and earnest and there was something sweet about her slight frame that Bea found endearing.

"Hi, Mrs Rushton. I didn't think you'd be coming back in today."

"Just made it," Bea said. "How's everything? It looks like you've got it all under control."

"It's fine," Candace said. "So far, it's been a slow day. Not many tourists. One of your friends was here a few minutes ago. She said she'd check back in after she'd done her shopping. Sorry, I can't remember her name."

"Thank you, Candace," Bea said. Who could it have been? Evie was next door in the bookshop. Taya and Penny would be busy working.

She set about cleaning up the kitchen. Slow days were

perfect for deep cleaning. It gave her a chance to reorganise cupboards, change things up or simply get rid of any dust or grime that'd accumulated. There were few things as satisfying as getting a kitchen to shine with a bit of elbow grease, in Bea's opinion.

The time flew by, and before she knew it, the bell over the door jangled. She glanced up to see Taya stepping through, her long legs enclosed in a pair of tight black leggings, a flowing silk shirt draped over the top. She pulled a pair of dark sunglasses down the bridge of her nose and peered around the café until her gaze landed on Bea's face.

"There you are. I could've called, but I wanted to surprise you. I've come for a hot drink and a chat. Do you have time?"

"Perfect timing," Bea replied. "Come in—grab a seat. I'll be with you in a minute. Chai?"

"You know me well."

Bea mixed up the spices to make her renowned chai tea every week. She served it with scones. It was one of the specials she offered and had become something of a hit with the locals. With a dab of fresh cream in a small bowl on the side, she carried the tray to the table, and after kissing her friend on the cheek in greeting, she sat across from Taya.

She poured the tea into their cups while Taya fussed with her hair. "This wind has made such a mess."

Bea clucked her tongue. "Nonsense. You look as though you've arrived here directly from a fashion shoot."

Taya laughed. "That's ridiculous. But do go on..."

Bea rolled her eyes. "You know you're gorgeous. You don't need my affirmations."

Taya winked. "It's good to see you, honey. It's been too long. And I'm not talking to my parents at the moment, so I'm feeling a bit lonely."

"Why aren't you speaking to them?"

"No particular reason. They're in Europe right now. But

even if they weren't, I'd be avoiding them. It's not their fault, but I'm feeling really insecure about the inn and have no idea what I should do. That's partly why I came to see you. I don't know who to talk to. Usually I'd go to Dad, but I'm afraid to hear what he'd have to say."

"You think you know?" Bea asked as she added jam to her scone.

Taya sighed. "Fairly certain he'd tell me I'm not using my brain. I'm holding on to the business because it's sentimental, and he'd sell it. Because he always makes sound business decisions, not emotional ones."

"Well, it's a fair point. Although I understand why you feel the way you do."

Taya took a bite of scone and chewed thoughtfully. "The thing is, perhaps I'm still rebelling against the idea that Mum and Dad want to control me. It's how I felt as a teen, and even though they don't do anything to suggest they still have those designs on me, I treat them as though they do."

Bea swallowed. "That makes sense. We often find it hard to let go of the way our parents used to see us. I know I've had to think carefully about the way I speak to my dad since I moved back to the island. Sometimes I feel like that snarky teenaged girl all over again and have to remember I'm an adult and he has feelings." She laughed. "One of the first signs of maturity is realising your parents can be hurt by the things you say. It took me a while to learn that, I'm sorry to admit."

"You're right, of course." Taya tapped a fingernail against the tabletop. "I'm running out of money. No, that's not true. I've run out of money. A while ago."

Bea's eyebrows shot up. "Oh, honey, I'm so sorry."

Taya waved a hand in front of her face. "It's fine. I mean, it's not really, but what else can I say? It's a disaster, and my life is over? Because that's not really true either..."

"No, your life isn't over. Business is hard — I am the first to admit that. We've barely made a profit at all here. I'm hoping that will improve as time goes on. And I still haven't paid for all the renovations I made to the café. If I hadn't been able to draw on the money I made selling the house in Sydney, I'd never have been able to launch this business. I don't know how you've managed to run the inn on your own for over two decades. That's a major achievement."

Taya's eyes filled with tears. "And it's all for nothing."

"Not necessarily. It's given you a steady income and a place to raise your daughter."

"That's true." Taya sniffled as she fossicked around in her purse. Finally she pulled out a tissue and wiped her nose. "It did support me and Camden for a lot of years. Without the inn, I'd probably never have been able to live here on the island with her. I'd have had to move to the mainland or accept help from my parents, which I've always tried not to do."

"There's nothing shameful about accepting help from family," Bea said, setting down her scone. "You've raised a daughter on your own, you survived losing your husband, and that's a lot to deal with. You're the only child your parents have — if Dani needed my help, I'd be there in a flash. And I'd want her to let me help. It brings parents a lot of joy to do something for their children."

"I know that's true, but I find it challenging to accept help. When I was young, people always used to tell me that I wouldn't have to do anything with my life since I had rich parents — I could just coast and let them look after me. It made me so mad when they said that. I didn't want to coast. I wanted to stand on my own two feet."

"And you have."

"Mum and Dad didn't think I had it in me. When Todd died, they said Camden and I should move in with them. That I could work for Dad—they'd take care of me. But that made me all the more determined not to do it. I wanted to prove

115

them wrong for so long that now I don't know how to do anything different."

"Would it be the worst thing in the world to let your dad invest in the inn?" Bea asked.

Taya ran fingers through her hair. "I don't know. It feels as though it would be. But maybe I'm overreacting."

"What's the alternative?"

"Selling or shutting the place down. I don't see how I can reopen. I've used up my line of credit on renovations. I need guests, but I can't bring them in without staff."

"Can I be blunt with you?" Bea took a sip of tea, then set down the cup in its saucer.

"Please do," Taya replied, straightening in her chair. "I need advice. I'm caught up in my own circle of panic and have no idea what to do."

"Your dad must be close to retirement. There was a time when he hoped you'd take over his business. Right?"

Taya nodded, chewed on the end of a fingernail.

"Whatever happens, you'll inherit the entire thing because you're their only heir. This could be the perfect opportunity for you to learn the business from the ground up. To prepare yourself for the time when you'll take over."

"You make a good point..." Taya leaned forwards. "I think Dad's planning on selling when he retires. But he might change his mind."

"Would you want that?"

She bit down on her lower lip. "I don't know."

"Something to think about, then."

"Thanks, Bea. I knew I could count on you for insight and advice. I couldn't get my mind to slow down enough to be logical. But you're right — if Dad doesn't have to sell the company, maybe he wouldn't want to. I could ask him to invest in the inn, to make it part of his company. And who knows? Maybe one day, I'll be part of that company."

"It's worth considering."

"Times like this, I miss Todd."

"I know you do." Bea reached out a hand to squeeze Taya's.

"It's been decades, so most of the time, I'm fine on my own. But when it comes to making a big decision about the business we built and dreamed over together, I wish he was here to help me."

Sixteen

THE BLUE SHOAL Inn stood in darkness as the evening gloaming settled across the bay. Taya crossed her arms as she studied it from the edge of the empty swimming pool. It was beautiful. Especially with the golden light from the last rays of the sunset glittering across the roof. Construction was complete. Every single part of the inn shone or glowed from the remodel. It was perfect. Everything she'd hoped it would be. But she still couldn't open it. Couldn't afford the staff or the supplies she needed to get things running, and the bank wasn't willing to give her anything more than it already had. They'd done an analysis of her market share and weren't convinced she was a good risk for them to take.

With a sigh, she rubbed both hands over her face and turned to sit on the steps leading down to the beach. Her father's business, the *Paradise Resort*, lived up to its name even from where she sat. It was everything her inn wasn't. Luxurious, spacious, modern, high tech and no doubt booked to capacity. She still felt a lingering resentment when she recalled their conversations about his initial plans — she'd objected to him building in Blue Shoal. He'd reminded her that he'd held off for two decades out of respect for her business, but he'd bought the land before she'd purchased the inn and it was time to do something with it. Not to mention the fact that he'd been a resident of the bay for longer than she'd been alive and he wanted to have a resort close to home where he could keep an eye on it.

She understood his reasoning. It made a lot of sense. But it wasn't any easier for her to deal with. And it still smarted that he hadn't considered her success in his plans. She wondered whether her inn could've survived in the current climate if he'd chosen to build his behemoth resort elsewhere. There was no way for her to know. Customers had become more discerning in recent years — they wanted luxury, the best chefs, the most amazing spa experience, the highest star rating. She'd seen the writing on the wall years ago, really. But she hadn't been willing to face the reality that the world had changed but her inn was still the same cosy, inviting, retro-inspired old lady it had always been. And now it'd had a face-lift, but would only ever attract a small niche of holidaymakers.

With one last glance over her shoulder at the dark, silent inn, she tramped down the steps and along the beach. The sand was cold on her feet. The air felt damp and chill. Small waves lapped quietly at the shoreline. The hill ahead of her was black against the deep blue sky, apart from the white buildings that made up the Paradise Resort.

It didn't take her long to locate Andrew's office. It was behind the reception area but had a private entrance, which she took. There was no need for the reception staff to see her and wonder what she was doing there. She wasn't even sure herself why she'd come. Only, she'd seen the resort in the distance and headed in that direction, almost as though the sirens had beckoned her there.

She knocked on the door even as her heart beat a staccato

rhythm against her ribcage. It took a moment for him to answer, and she'd turned away thinking he wasn't there when she heard his voice.

"Taya?"

She spun to face him, her cheeks burning hot. "Hi, Andrew. I thought you'd gone home. I didn't want to bother you. Just came to check and see how the dog is faring."

He ushered her into the office and onto a large, soft couch along one wall. She couldn't help admiring the space. It was large and perfectly decorated with a sitting area, a sturdy timber desk, and long windows that overlooked the tropical gardens behind the resort.

"Daisy is fine. I found her owners the next day. Someone spotted my flyer at the corner shop and gave me a call. They were very happy to have her back."

"I hope you told them it's irresponsible not to have her microchipped."

"I mentioned something about that. They assured me they'd get it done right away. It was pretty upsetting to them. She'd been gone for two nights, I believe."

"I'm glad it all worked out," Taya replied, suddenly feeling awkward. She ran both hands down the front of her pants as if to smooth out nonexistent wrinkles.

"It's nice to see you again," he said. "How's the inn coming along?"

There was really no way to avoid the truth. They'd find out soon enough when she didn't reopen. Besides, her parents would be back in Blue Shoal the following week. She couldn't hide her failure from them forever.

She swallowed. "It looks fantastic. The contractor has done a great job. But unfortunately I'm experiencing a cash flow problem."

"Oh?" He crossed one leg over the other.

"As in... I have none." She cleared her throat. "And I need some in order to reopen."

"That is a problem." His eyes narrowed. "Have you thought any more about my proposal? I meant what I said, I'd like to buy your inn and add it to your father's portfolio. It would complement the Paradise Resort perfectly."

"I have thought about it, and I'm interested. I've decided that I'd like to give Dad a chance to purchase the inn, but I'll need to talk to him about it first."

"I think that's a great idea. He will be a better investor for you than anyone else could. Do you have plans for what you might do?"

She hesitated. "I don't know. Honestly, the hospitality industry is the only business I've ever known. I'm good at it, too. But I don't know if I could work for someone else. I love the idea of building my own legacy."

"You could help build your family's legacy," he offered.

"You're the second person to mention that today."

"Then it must be a good idea." He laughed. "I'd love to offer you the assistant manager position here at the Paradise Resort. I've been looking for several weeks and haven't found anyone suitable. If you would like to, you can work alongside myself and my staff to learn the ropes around here. You can help to find a manager for your inn as well, unless you'd prefer to take on that role yourself."

He leaned back and rested an arm along the top of the couch. Suddenly she felt so tired. It was exhausting to keep going with the level of anxiety she'd held in her body in recent weeks.

"I'd love to take the job. And I'd also be happy to find a replacement manager for the inn. I think I've filled that role long enough. Thank you, Andrew. I know you didn't have to do that. I hope my father will be okay with it."

"He will be thrilled," Andrew said.

"If he and I can come to an agreement, then I'm happy to move forward," she replied.

He leapt to his feet and held out a hand. She stood slowly and shook it.

"Let's celebrate," he said. He glanced around the office then hurried to a cupboard and opened it. He shut it and opened another. "I have a bottle of gin around here somewhere. I don't often drink, and someone gave it to me as a gift. I stuck it in one of these cupboards. Oh, here it is." He pulled out a bottle and held it aloft. "Now I have to find some glasses."

He poked his head out through the door to where his assistant sat and asked her for two glasses. She returned in less than a minute and passed them to Andrew, giving Taya a curious side glance.

Andrew opened the bottle with a quiet pop and poured the gin into the glasses, topped them up with tonic water from a small fridge beside his desk, even as Taya's head spun. Had she done the right thing? Did she really have any other choice? This was the best option. The wisest business decision. After all, like Bea had pointed out, one day this might all be hers, along with the rest of her father's portfolio. Unless he sold it off before then. Maybe if she did the job well, she'd be able to convince him not to break up the business when he retired.

Andrew set the bottle on a small coffee table with an enormous book of Scottish castles on it and handed her a glass. "Let's drink to our future business endeavour and to great success for the Paradise Company and the Eldridge family."

She raised her glass. "And to you as well, Andrew."

They tapped their glasses together and both drank at the same time. The bubbles tickled her nose, and the sweet flavour burst across her tongue, making her giddy before the drink had even reached her stomach. Or perhaps it was Andrew's closeness that had her head spinning, or the enormous career decision she'd made so spontaneously. Whatever it was, she felt light — as though a huge weight had been lifted from her shoulders and the knot in her stomach had been replaced by a swirling mass of butterflies.

"I'm so grateful for this opportunity," she said. "I won't let you down."

He stepped closer to her, his deep brown eyes drawing her in, his gaze traveling over her face to linger at her lips. She licked them slowly, her heart hammering.

"I..." Before she could say another word, he'd reached for her with his free hand and pulled her close. His face hovered over hers, his hand splayed across her lower back. Her body was pressed to his, and she could feel his warmth through her thin silk shirt. Then he kissed her, and his full, soft lips stole every thought from her mind.

He moved slowly, as if in a steady beating rhythm with her heart, his mouth exploring hers in a way that made her forget where she was. This couldn't be happening. It wasn't right. He'd offered her a job only moments earlier. A job she very much needed. This would ruin her chance of becoming part of her father's business, of saving her inn, of saving herself.

"No, we can't..." she said, stepping back and pulling herself out of his embrace.

"I'm sorry," he stammered, his eyes bright. "I didn't mean..."

"It's not your fault. It was both of us. We had a moment, that's all. But we're going to be working together, and I don't want to jeopardise that." She spun around and ran out through the private door and down the narrow, winding path away from the resort.

Seventeen

PENNY CLOSED the small black door on her post office box and lifted the envelope up to peer at the return address. It was the DNA results she'd requested. She had to know for certain Buck was her father. There was no way her mother would lie about something like that, but in order to have certainty when she next spoke to Buck, she needed proof, and this letter was that.

With her pulse racing and a cold sweat beneath her summer dress, she walked from the post office to a small park across the street and sat on a bench. With a slow intake of breath, she slipped a finger under the lip of the envelope and tore it open.

There was a single sheet of paper inside. It confirmed what she already believed — Buck was her biological father. Her throat tightened. All these years, she'd wished she could know who her father was, to spend time with him, get to know him, find out if he liked the same things, if he shared her hair colour, and he was there on the island all along. Barely more than ten kilometres from her childhood home. It seemed wrong that her mother had kept this from her for so long.

And what about Buck? He had to know he was her father, yet he'd never reached out, never wanted to see her.

She took a walk around Kellyville and stopped in front of Betsy's Florals. Betsy was inside with Sam, her granddaughter. Since Buck was her biological father, that meant Betsy was her aunt. The thought filled her with warmth. If she was going to discover a long-lost aunt, there was no one better than Betsy Norton. The woman was practically picture-perfect with her array of colourful silk kaftans, her wild grey curls and her sparkling blue eyes. Penny hadn't seen her or Sam in a while, so she pushed open the door and stepped inside.

"Hi there," she called, waving to Sam.

Sam ran over to give her a hug. "I'm painting. Do you want to paint with me?" She had a dab of blue paint on her cheek and a streak of red in her hair. She was dressed in her school uniform with a paint smock over the top.

Penny laughed. "Let me see what you're painting." Sam took her by the hand and led her to a small desk beside Betsy's own much larger one. On it was a vibrantly coloured picture of the ocean, with various fish swimming around and a large tree beside a bright yellow beach.

"Wow, I love it. Very colourful," Penny said. She squatted beside the desk as Sam continued to explain every aspect of the painting in great detail.

It was clear to Penny how much the two of them were thriving in each other's company. Sam looked like a different girl, so neat and clean. Betsy gazed lovingly at her grand-daughter as she prattled on about rainbow-coloured fish and anemone, which she mispronounced delightfully.

Betsy was arranging native flowers in a crystal vase. Finally, when Sam stopped to draw breath, she spoke up. "It's nice to see you today, honey. What are you doing in town?"

Penny stood to her feet. It took a lot more effort than it used to, and there was an ache in her hip that was new. Sometimes it felt like she was still twenty years old, and on other days, she wondered if she should start browsing the internet for her first walking stick.

She leaned against Betsy's desk and spoke quietly so Sam wouldn't hear. "She looks like she's settling in nicely."

Betsy snipped the end off a bottlebrush flower. "She's an absolute delight. We have a wonderful time together. I can't thank you enough for helping me build a bridge with my family."

"How are things going with your son?"

"He still won't talk to me other than about Sam. He acknowledges that he needs help with her, and he's happy for me to step in and do that. But he doesn't want to reconcile." Betsy's expression didn't betray any emotion, but Penny knew she must've felt her son's rejection keenly.

"I'm sure he'll come around," Penny said. "Just give it time."

"I should never have said anything," Betsy replied, pausing in her work to study her granddaughter's profile. "I told him I didn't think his girlfriend was a good match for him, that she didn't have the character to make a marriage work. He married her and never forgave me for what I said."

Penny shook her head. "I'm so sorry. I bet it's hard to know what to say as a parent. Especially if you have reservations about someone."

"It was impossible at the time. I saw what he was getting himself into... Turns out I was right. Although I take no pleasure in the fact. She left them both a couple of years ago, but he never said a word to me about it."

"And that's the reason for the conflict in your relationship?"

"That and a few other things," Betty said. "I do the best I can, but I'm human. I have flaws. Sometimes I fail myself, and sometimes I fail my family. But everything I've ever done has been to protect him. Unfortunately, he can't see that. I've lived for him, I've lied for him, I've done everything a mother could do. He's in his fifties now. I think it's time I let it all go and wait for him to come to me. I'd hoped as he grew older, he'd realise that family matters enough to fight for it, but he's taking longer than most."

It must've been hard to watch her son from a distance. To miss all the major milestones in his life. To wait for that phone call or a knock on the door. Penny's heart ached for all the things Betsy longed for but couldn't have. At least she'd helped bring Betsy and Sam back together.

"I'm sorry, Betsy. I know that must be hard for you. I know my mother has done things that I don't always understand. It's hard, but I choose to forgive her because she's important to me. And because she was so young..." She wanted to tell Betsy about their connection, but didn't know how to get the conversation started. It was such a strange thing to say, especially when they'd known each other her whole life but as acquaintances, nothing more.

"He's still mad about the alibi, you know."

"What?" Penny's mind struggled to catch up with Betsy's rapid U-turn.

"Remember we talked about how I was Buck's alibi after your grandmother's murder?"

"Yes, of course. Why would your son be angry about that?"

Betsy returned to her work, angrily clipping flower stems and sliding the flowers into the vase one by one. "It's a mystery. Honestly, I have no idea what goes through his mind. But he knows how I feel about family. We stick together through thick and thin. We don't give up on each other because times get tough. Buck and I—we've been through some stuff together, let me tell you. Things no one else knows about. Buck's always been there for me, so I was for him. It's as simple as that."

Penny's brow furrowed. What was she saying? Had Betsy lied to cover for her brother? No, it couldn't be true. If she asked the question, Betsy would be mortified. She wasn't the kind of person to tell a lie, let alone to the police. As long as she'd known the woman, she'd seen her strength of character, her integrity.

Once, when Penny was in her twenties, Betsy had found a tourist's money belt and had taken it directly to the police to hand in. The owner had offered her a finder's reward, and she'd turned them down. Then, when they insisted, she used the money to buy everyone in the pub on the corner a round of drinks. Everyone on the island remembered that story. She was well-known in their community, and well-loved.

Penny cleared her throat. "On the subject of your brother, I have some news."

Betsy paused in her work, one eyebrow quirked. "Oh?"

"He's my biological father. Apparently your relationship with him isn't the only one he's kept a secret all these years."

Betsy's face grew pale, and she leaned against the bench, swaying slightly. "My dear, what did you say?"

"You're my aunt. Surprise, it's a girl!" Penny attempted to make light of the situation with a bright voice and by throwing her hands in the air as if she danced at a cabaret, but her voice wobbled.

Betsy's eyes widened. "Well, I never."

Eighteen

BEA STUBBED her toe on a rock and sat down in the sand with a grunt. She studied the injured toe and found it was bleeding. The sand was wet, and seeped into her shorts. She got to her feet and hobbled to the place where the walkway to the cottage met the beach and sat on a low, flat rock instead. Then she checked the toe again. The damage was minimal, the bleeding already abated.

Her breathing had returned to normal. She was attempting a longer walk with more uphill sections than usual. She'd climbed up a hill beyond the cottage through tall, spindly seagrasses by patches of pandanus and scrub. The entire hill was pockmarked with chunks of porous sandstone hidden beneath the waving grasses and half covered with blown sand. It was easy enough not to see it in time to avoid kicking it. But if she was going to deviate away from the beach, she'd remember to wear walking shoes next time.

While she was still examining her toe, a movement caught her attention in her periphery. She looked up and saw nothing but the swaying branches of a small she-oak, then the top of the black rocks beyond that overlooked the ocean.

In the distance, there was another movement. Something dark darting between shrubs and trees in the shadows. She raised a hand to shield her face from the glare of the sun and did her best to focus on whatever it was. A dark figure, a human — she was sure of it. The person walked steadily, head down, clothed from top to bottom in dark fabric. They blended into the thick scrub as they scuttled away from the rocky cliff top.

Why hadn't she seen them stark against the rocks? Perhaps they'd come around the side of the hill facing away from her. That would mean they'd been down to the ocean's edge where there was no beach, no sand. Why would anyone go down there? Unless perhaps they'd come by boat and were stranded.

She stood to her feet and set off in the direction of the cliff top. If there was a boat anchored nearby, it could be in trouble. There was nowhere to safely land, and perhaps she could call for help — she had her phone in her pocket. Within minutes, she'd reached the top of the cliffs and peered out over the sparkling azure waters below.

It was a bright sunny day, and the light glinted off the sea as it undulated gently under a light breeze. There was no sign of a boat. But thinking about a boat reminded her of the day she'd test-driven her own boat. This was very close to the location where she'd seen that hidden cave. It was impossible to spot now from where she was standing, but had been visible from the ocean. Was it possible the shadowy figure had visited the cave?

A shiver ran over her, setting goose pimples rising along her arms and legs. She glanced back in the direction the person had gone and saw no sign of them. They'd disappeared into the thick bush. The road wasn't far away, and it was likely they were parked nearby.

But why had they visited the cave? If that was what they'd done. Curiosity ate at her while she stood there. What would it hurt for her to take a look? It was her imagination running wild and too many evenings spent watching *CSI*, no doubt. Nothing exciting ever happened on Coral Island. But what if there was something that she'd missed? She'd lived here for much of her young life and never even realised the cave existed.

With a stab of anxiety in her chest, she began the descent down and around the side of the hill that led to the cliffs. The cliffs themselves were tall and craggy, black rocks that looked as though they'd taken a tumble and formed a vertical wedge in the earth. But the side of the cliffs sloped easily down to the ocean, and there was something of a natural path on seagrass and between large, porous rocks.

After a while, she had to use both hands to navigate through the rocks, now closer together and more mountainous. Then she was climbing up and down, clambering over rocks and around them until finally she found herself standing within reach of the water. It lapped softly against the rocks in some places and threw itself with a crash in others, leaving white foam in a layer close to the cliff face.

Sea salt sprayed her in a gentle mist as another wave dashed against the cliff face. Then she climbed in a hurry, before the next set arrived, towards where she believed the cave would be. It was no surprise she'd never seen the entrance before, since it was so well hidden that she didn't spy it until she was standing before it.

With wide eyes, she inched forwards. The cave mouth was narrow, both horizontally and vertically. She had to duck her head to go inside, and this gave her another rush of adrenaline as fear coursed through her veins. Should she go inside when the waves were so close to entering the cave? She wouldn't stay long—no doubt the tide was rising, and the last thing she wanted was to be caught in a deep, dark cave by rushing water.

The darkness threw her off at first. She stopped and blinked a few moments, allowing her eyes to adjust after the glare from outside. Then, she saw a cosy-looking shallow cave with a sand floor ahead of her. She stepped forwards onto the sand, glad of the relief for her feet, which had become quite sore from traipsing over the sharp black rocks outside and in the cave's mouth.

The sand was cold and wet against her feet. She walked forwards, suddenly realising she had no idea why she'd come or what she was looking for. There was nothing in the cave. It wasn't nearly as scary or as mysterious as it'd seemed looking in from beyond the waves. It had dark, wet walls and a stretch of sand between them. Nothing more than that. There was a small rock pool on one side, and perhaps she might find a crayfish or some oysters there, but otherwise, the scramble down the hillside to find the cave had been a fruitless endeavour.

Then she noticed that some of the sand had been disturbed. She stepped forwards gingerly, studying it as closely as she could manage in the dull light. There were definitely footprints in the sand. The person she'd seen in the shadows had been there after all. But why? What would bring someone down to this hidden cave?

The sound of a rock falling down the cliff face startled her and set her heart racing. She looked out over her shoulder at the blue of the ocean and the brightness of the sky within the dark mouth of the cave. It looked as though it was yawning and might close at any moment. The thought sent a shudder through her. She was being ridiculous and letting her imagination run wild. She'd give herself a panic attack if she didn't calm down.

With a shake of her head, she turned her attention back to the footprints — they'd definitely been made by someone wearing a pair of boots. Maybe work boots or something similar. They were medium-sized prints with deep furrows from the tread pattern. She followed them deeper into the cave, hunching down lower as the ceiling sloped down on her.

The patch of sand at her feet looked as though it'd been dug up and patted back into place. There were handprints all over it, and the sand was messy, unlike the neatly packed sand that covered the rest of the space.

With a frown, she got down on her hands and knees and dug at the sand with her fingertips. It came up easily, as loose as it was. And within moments, her fingernails came into contact with something hard.

"Ouch!" she exclaimed, pulling her hands back a moment. Had she hit a rock? Surely the sand wasn't so shallow.

This time more carefully, she continued digging and pushed the sand aside. There was something dark but most definitely not porous rock. It looked like black metal. She dug around the edges and then pulled it free. It was some kind of box — rectangular with a lock on the front of it. It was rusted in places and looked old. One corner of the lid didn't quite fit in place properly, and there was a dent in the top.

Another rock blundered down the outside of the cave. This time, it was larger and landed in the water with a splash. Bea's heart skipped a beat, and she leapt to her feet with a muffled cry. There was no reason for her to stay in that cave any longer than she had to. Every little thing was setting her nerves on edge. But if she took the box with her, the person who'd left it there would know she'd been there.

She covered the sand back over the hole and patted it down with her hands the way it'd been before. With her head on one side, she studied it closely — that looked about right. Any cursory glance would appear as though the box was still buried. But if someone tried to dig it up, they'd quickly know it wasn't there. She'd have to return it just as soon as she figured out how to open it.

Was she really doing this? It wasn't any of her business what someone had hidden in a cave inside a metal box. It might've been a kid burying a secret treasure or putting aside trinkets for his or her future self to discover later, like a time capsule. Although the footprints were too large for it to have been a small child.

If it was a time capsule, she wouldn't disturb the box's contents. She'd put it back exactly as she'd found it. Although she doubted it would last long in the cave once the tide rose, but that wasn't her responsibility. Still, her curiosity wouldn't let her leave it there.

With the box under one arm, she hurried out of the cave and up the side of the hill. She was breathing heavily by the time she reached the top. With a quick look around to make sure the person who'd hidden the box hadn't returned, she ducked her head and ran in the direction of the cottage. Dad had some bolt cutters at home; she would open the box and find out what was inside.

* * *

When she reached her father's house, Bea was red-faced and bathed in sweat. The hill the house was built on was the highest on the island apart from the single mountain at its centre, Mount Prospect. She trudged the last few steps up the driveway, one hand pressed to her hip, the other still cupping the metal box to her side.

"Why ... did ... you ... build ... here?" she asked Dad, leaning against the doorframe when he opened it.

He arched an eyebrow in surprise. "The view... What's going on? Did you run up? Are you okay?"

She stepped inside and held up the metal box. "Gotta get inside."

"I'm going to need full sentences," Dad said as he shut the door behind her.

"Water."

"That's not a sentence."

Bea glowered at him.

He laughed. "Come on, I'll get you a drink. Maybe then you'll be able to do more than grunt at me."

She followed him into the kitchen, her breathing easing all the time. Finally, she sat at the bench and chugged down a glass of water. She set it on the bench top. "Much better."

Dad sipped his own glass. "Okay, now you can talk again — what's the box for? Why did you run here?"

She eyed the box on the dining table where she'd left it. "I found it in that little cave down near the cottage."

"What cave?"

"There's a cave in the cliff face. You can really only see it from the ocean."

"Oh, yeah, I know what you mean. I've seen it before, but it didn't look like much more than an indentation in the rocks."

"It's a cave."

"Interesting."

"I saw it when I was test-driving my boat with Brad. Anyway, this morning I was taking a walk around the headland when I saw someone come up the hill from that direction. The only thing I could think of was the cave, so I went there to take a look."

"Why?" Dad's brow was furrowed. "What does it matter if they were walking by the cave?"

"It's not exactly an easy stroll. Why would they be down there? They were dressed in black, Dad."

He raised both hands in mock surrender. "Oh, dear. They were dressed in black. Forgive me. Go on."

She rolled her eyes. "You have no sense of mystery, Dad."

He laughed. "You have enough for both of us. Finish the story, please."

"So, I went into the cave..."

"The tide is turning. That wasn't a very clever thing to do."

"Dad, you're interrupting a lot."

"Sorry, keep going. Just don't go into an ocean cave when the tide is turning again. Okay?"

"Okay, you got it. I won't do it again."

"Thank you."

She cleared her throat. "Can I continue?"

"Yes, please. I don't know what's taking you so long." His eyes twinkled.

She shook her head. "Anyhoo, I went into the cave and saw that the sand on the ground was disturbed. So, I dug around a bit, and I found this." She pointed to the box.

"Really?" Dad crossed his arms. "That's intriguing. What's in it?"

"I have no idea. That's why I'm here. I thought you might be able to help me open it."

"It's not yours."

"I know it's not mine. But I'm going to put it back. I just want to make sure it's..."

"It's what?"

Her cheeks flushed with warmth. "You know, that it's not... Oh, forget it. I'm nosy, okay? I want to know what's inside and why someone would go to all that trouble."

Dad tutted with his tongue. "Curiosity killed the cat."

"I'm not a cat, so I'm fine. Can you open it or not?"

"Of course I can. I'll get my bolt cutters and be right back."

He returned five minutes later and soon had the lock removed from the box. Then he stepped aside so Bea could open it. Since the lid was lopsided and dinged on top, it took a bit of wriggling back and forth, but it finally popped open.

Bea reached inside and pulled items out one at a time. There was a T-shirt rolled into a ball, a photograph and some

138

kind of ID card. She set them all on the table, then picked up the shirt to look at it more closely. It was a shirt, small and very old.

"A shirt?" she said. "And it's stained."

"That's not a shirt. That's a blouse," Dad said.

Bea chewed on her cheek. "You're right. How do you know that, Dad?"

"I've been around a while."

"You're full of surprises."

"I try to keep you on your toes. That looks like blood to me."

"Blood?" Bea's goose bumps were back, this time across her entire body.

"Yep. Blood gets dark like that after a while. This is a very old, bloodstained blouse."

Bea set the blouse on the table and reached for the photo. It was old too. Yellowed and stained. In the image, a young girl smiled up at the photographer, shy and happy.

"She looks familiar," Dad said, brow furrowed. "I think that's Penny's mother, Ruby. It's hard to say because the photo is in such bad shape, but it looks like her."

A shiver ran up Bea's spine. "Why would someone bury a bloody blouse along with a photograph of Penny's mother in a sandy cave?"

"Not for any good reason. What's this?"

He picked up the ID badge. It was a piece of thin cardboard, laminated. It read:

California Driver's License
    Expires on birthday 1975
    Samuel Jay Gilmore

. . .

The photograph was of a young man with thick blond hair combed forwards in the 1970s style. He wore a striped button-down shirt and sported a sandy-blonde, swooping moustache.

"Who is that?" Bea asked, peering at it.

Dad looked more closely. "I should go and get my glasses. Where are they?"

"On top of your head," Bea replied without looking at him.

He patted his head, found the glasses and pushed them down onto his nose. "Well, I'll be... That's Buck Clements."

Nineteen

DAD WAITED for Bea to shower and change at the cottage before the two of them drove up to the police station in Kellyville. Harry was napping in his bedroom, so she didn't bother to wake him.

Her heart hammered in her chest. This was big. Possibly very big. What would the police say? Would they believe her? Would she get into trouble? There was no way of knowing how it would play out, but she had to do the right thing and hand in the items she'd found. They might be the very thing the police needed to finally crack the case of Penny's grandmother's murder.

Dad parked his truck outside the police station. It was a small office on one of the few streets in the main part of town. It was brick with a blue-and-white sign that announced "Coral Island Police" in bold letters.

As they climbed out of the car, Bea held the box tight against her side.

"Hey, Bea. What are you doing here?"

Penny's voice caught her by surprise, and she almost dropped the box. The last person she wanted to see in that moment was her friend. The probability that Penny's newly discovered father might in fact be the murderer they'd all wondered about wasn't exactly something Bea looked forward to passing on.

"Oh, Penny, what a lovely surprise. Just taking a walk with Rob, are you? Good to see you, Rob."

Penny and her brother stood side by side. Penny had a look of confusion on her face. "Aren't you going into the station?"

Bea's cheeks flamed. "Um... Well..."

"We are indeed," Dad said. Bea shook her head in a plea for him to be quiet. His eyes narrowed as though questioning her sanity.

"We are too. What a coincidence."

"What are you here for?" Bea asked.

Penny glanced at Rob, who nodded as if to encourage her. "I was talking to Betsy a few days ago, and she said something that bothered me. She said she'd lied for family, that it's what family did for one another. I wondered if maybe she'd lied about her alibi for Buck. It's hard to explain, and maybe I'm making something out of nothing, but I thought I should tell the police my suspicions. They'll probably laugh me out of the station. But I couldn't stop thinking about it. So, here I am. What about you?"

Bea hesitated. "I'm here about Buck as well."

* * *

Inside the police station, both Bea and Penny took turns giving their statements. Bea turned in the evidence she'd located in the cave. Finally, hours later, they all emerged from the office, exhausted and ready to move on.

Dad had already gone home to check on Harry, so Bea called him to return and pick her up. She stood on the curb beside Penny while she waited. Rob had gone down the street to buy bread and milk.

"I'm sorry I had to do that," Bea said.

"Why are you sorry?"

"You only found out Buck was your dad a few days ago, and now I'm turning him in to the police for a possible murder."

"If he killed my grandmother, he shouldn't get away with it. I don't care that he's my dad, I want the truth to come out."

"Do you believe he did it?" Bea asked.

Penny shook her head slowly. "I don't know. The evidence certainly is suspicious, at the very least. I don't know how he'll explain that driver's licence. Who is he? What's his real name? Is it the name on the licence, or the name he uses now?"

"And the bloody shirt..."

"That was definitely spooky," Penny admitted. "I'll have to call Mum when I get home and let her know what's happened."

"Do you think she'll be okay?"

Penny shrugged. "Who knows? I think the main reason she convinced Dad they should move away from the island was to get away from all of this. The murder haunted her for years. She never recovered."

"Completely understandable."

"Of course, but for me as a kid — it was hard to come to terms with it. She was here, but not really. Always so tense, worried about every little thing. Became something of a control freak. It's caused anxiety issues."

"I can see why." Bea slipped an arm around Penny's shoulders and gave her a sideways squeeze. "Maybe this will allow you both some closure finally."

"I hope so," Penny replied.

Twenty

TAYA HELD the mobile phone aloft so the camera could take in the sight of the Blue Shoal Inn behind her.

"There it is," she said.

Her daughter, Camden, was on a video call with her. "It looks great, Mum. You've all done a fantastic job."

"Thanks, sweetie. I wish you were here in person to see it."

"I know. I'll try to come for a visit soon, but it's hard to get away. Chef won't give me any time off right now, plus I'm studying every spare moment I get."

"I understand." Taya didn't want to sound like a whiny toddler, but sometimes she felt like crying when she thought about how long it'd been between her daughter's visits.

"Don't get upset, Mum," Camden said. She'd always been able to read Taya like a book. "Now that you've sold the inn to Grandpa, maybe you can visit me instead."

"That's true," Taya mused. "I'm footloose and fancy free. No responsibilities to weigh me down."

A month had passed since she'd offered the inn to Andrew at their meeting. Her parents had returned from Europe only days later, and she'd met with her father to discuss terms. In the end, she'd been very happy with the arrangement, and her father was over the moon. He'd hugged her and told her he was proud of her. His response had helped her feel more confident in her decision.

"It's a family business," Dad had said. "And now you can be the one to take it to the next level."

"You haven't retired yet, Dad," she'd objected.

"No, but it won't be long. I've had enough. I was holding off because I hated to sell it after all the work I've put in. But now that you're coming on board, I can finally let go. I know you'll do a fantastic job. I've watched you run your inn over the years. You know the business well."

"But I failed..." she said, her stomach tightening into a knot.

"No, you didn't. The market changed, and you're flexing with it. That's not failure."

"True," she said. She hadn't closed her inn; she'd accepted a good offer for it. Perhaps that's what business looked like — shifting and changing with the times, but never giving up. Life too.

"Are you ready?" Camden asked.

Taya set the phone on a stone wall beside the small rose garden that she'd built beside the inn as a kind of memorial to Todd after he died. The roses had budded, and some had begun to bloom. It was late spring on the island, and already the heat of the changing season was in the air.

"Can you see?" she asked.

"I think we should start with a prayer."

Taya let Camden lead the way. Her daughter's new faith was something of a surprise to her, but she enjoyed the sound of the words as they surrounded her like a warm embrace. They each spoke about the inn, about Todd and how much they missed him. Camden didn't remember him, but Taya had told her stories about him so many times, she felt as though she did.

Taya had sold the inn. It was no longer in her name, but belonged to her father's company. The family company. In that respect, she still owned it, in a way. But it was the end of an era. She'd no longer be at the inn's beck and call. If someone was sick and unable to work, it wouldn't be Taya who'd have to fill in. She wouldn't spend nights and weekends sitting in the small office in front of her old computer screen, clacking away at the keys as she paid bills and made orders. Someone else would be filling that role.

The more she thought about it, the more it excited her. The prospect of doing something new with her life, something meaningful, was out there — the world was full of possibility for the first time in decades. And there was a buzz in her gut that had her head spinning whenever she gave herself a chance to think about it.

It'd been Camden's idea to hold a farewell ceremony. "It's important to mark the end of one era and the beginning of a new one. We have to acknowledge it."

Taya had agreed, and now she was glad of her daughter's insight. Tears filled the corners of her eyes as she retold a familiar story about the inn almost falling down around them one night during a particularly bad cyclone, during which the guests had helped to nail the windows shut and bring in all the outdoor furniture.

They'd ended up sodden, cold and huddled in the dark living room until Taya had lit the fire and Camden had helped her serve everyone hot chocolate from the gas stove, along with cold cuts of meat on bread they'd baked earlier that morning. It'd been terrifying at the time, but was now one of Taya's favourite memories. Because they'd managed — just the two of them — to hold it all together, to keep everyone calm and to rebuild after the damage the storm inflicted. That was back when they'd lived onsite. Camden had grown up there. They'd been a family within those walls.

To finish the ceremony, they each lit a small candle. Taya in the rose garden, beneath the sloping canopy of climbing vines overhead, and Camden in her flat in Cairns. Then, they said goodbye. There were still tears in Taya's eyes as she hung up the phone and turned to leave. Andrew stood at the gate to the garden, his hands in his pockets, his head hanging low.

"Oh, hi," she said.

He offered her a sad smile. "Sorry. I didn't mean to pry or to interrupt."

"It's okay," she said. "I don't mind. We're saying goodbye. This inn was a dream my husband and I had a long time ago, and I've been reluctant to embrace change because of him. I should've sold it when I had the chance years ago."

"You're sad about moving on. I get it."

"No," she replied, stepping towards him. "I'm not really. It's emotional because it's a final goodbye, but the truth is, I've let this inn hold me back. It was a great way to support my daughter while she lived at home, but she's an adult now. I've always wanted to travel, see the world, make a difference, but instead I stayed put while other people travelled here and told me about their adventures. Now I can have some of those adventures myself."

"I'm glad to hear it. I was worried you'd regret your choice."

"I'm feeling free for the first time in as long as I can remember. I know I've got a job to do, but I don't think it will hold me back as much as the inn has done. This place will always be special to me. It's a part of who I am, but it's time for me to move on."

"That sounds very healthy."

It was the first time they'd seen each other since their kiss. The tension between them made Taya's feet itch to leave, but she stayed where she was, waiting for him to address it. Instead, he offered her a wan smile, waved goodbye and walked away. She watched him go in disbelief — did he plan to completely ignore their chemistry and the incident in his office?

* * *

Two days later, on Monday morning, Taya showed up to the Paradise Resort offices for her first day. She was nervous, like she was going back to school after the summer break. She knew most of the people who worked there, but still, she felt out of place. This wasn't her homely little inn; this was a giant resort.

She stepped into the reception area and took a seat. While she waited for the receptionist to get off the phone, she watched people flit through the offices, back and forth, here and there. Everyone had a job to do, and they moved like clockwork. The resort was clearly well-managed, there was little drama, and everyone simply got on with what they had to do.

She had to admit, it was a well-oiled machine compared to her small-time inn. She hoped it would become a second home to her the way the inn had. But for now, it was a strange, imposing place that made her more than a little anxious that she might not live up to their expectations. After all, she was the boss's daughter — she had big shoes to fill.

Finally, the receptionist turned her attention to Taya, and once she realised who she was, gave her a very warm welcome. She led her through the office to meet the office manager, a buxom woman named Dana with a perfectly styled grey bun and large green eyes. Dana showed Taya around the office, set her up in a cubicle, and had her fill out a ream of paperwork. By the time lunch rolled around, Taya had a throbbing headache and was ready to go home and put her feet up. She'd met so many people, attended her first meeting and completed more forms than ever before in her life — at least it seemed that way.

"Would you like to come to the restaurant with us for lunch?" Dana asked, poking her head around the wall of Taya's cubicle.

"That sounds nice," Taya said. She hadn't packed a lunch that morning—she'd been too nervous. But now her stomach was clenched tight with hunger and her head was light.

Taya, Dana and a few of the other office staff—whose names had already flown out of Taya's overwhelmed head—all walked together to the restaurant. They found a table in a back room and ordered off the menu. Taya ordered the chicken Parmesan and sat back to listen to the chatter from the group. It was always interesting to start in a new office and observe the dynamics especially since no one there seemed to have any idea who she was, other than a new employee.

She recognised one of the women as Andrew's assistant from her last visit to the resort. The woman's name turned out to be Sally. She was young, maybe late twenties, thin and full of vivacity. She hardly stopped speaking to draw breath, and her face expressed a wide range of emotions all in the space of a single sentence.

"Where are you from?" Dana asked Taya once conversation had died down.

"I'm from Blue Shoal. I used to own the Blue Shoal Inn."

"Oh, yeah. I thought I recognised you," Sally said. "Mr Reddy bought your inn, didn't he?"

"That's right. And he gave me a job, too."

"Oh, okay," Dana said. The atmosphere at the table changed imperceptibly. Suddenly she was one of the management team, and the casual banter was replaced by an awkward silence.

"I'm heading back to work. Lovely to meet you all." She stood to her feet and made her way out of the restaurant and into a hallway that would take her back to the office. There was no need for them to stop enjoying their lunch simply because she was there with them. No doubt that would be her last lunch invitation. She knew how it worked—it'd always been that way at her own inn. The staff there had loved her, but whenever they got together, she gave them space so they could relax and have fun.

As soon as she stepped into the hall, she collided with Andrew, who was reading a report and not looking where he was going.

"Oh, sorry!"

He placed a hand on her shoulder to steady her. "Never mind—it's my fault. I should pay more attention." His hand dropped to his side. The other clutched the papers he'd been distracted by. "First day?"

"That's right," she said.

"I was just reading through this job description for a position we need to fill in the head office. It looks interesting. They want to hire someone to go from location to location, opening new resorts and checking in with managers to ensure everything's on track, they're conforming to the brand, and they don't have any major issues. Basically to keep the lines of communication open."

"That does sound interesting. Where would the position be located?"

"Cairns," he replied. "Although I suppose it could be from anywhere, since there's travel involved and we have video conferencing."

"I'd like to be considered for the job," she said, surprising herself with the words.

His eyes widened. "What? Really?"

"Yes. I've wanted to travel for as long as I can remember,

151

but I've hardly been anywhere. This would give me a chance to do that and to get to know the business on a different level."

"That makes sense," he replied. "I hadn't thought of you. I should've."

"It's okay. I've been pondering another program I'd like to discuss further when you get the chance. I'm interested in mentoring and coaching women in all our locations to take the needed steps to get into management positions. What do you think?"

He gaped. "Uh, yeah. I like the idea a lot. You'd be willing to do that?"

"I'd love it," she replied. "It would give me a chance to meaningfully contribute to the company while learning the ropes."

"Let's meet about that soon. You can set something up with Sally."

"Okay, will do." What she wanted in that moment was for him to kiss her. But that would be completely unprofessional. Still, he was so close to her, his lips so inviting. And she'd been the one to pull away the last time, to tell him they shouldn't do it. Perhaps she was wrong.

"I'll see you later," he said.

He walked away, and she kicked herself for not speaking up. She was an adult, he was too, and they were both single. She should say something to him about their kiss, ask him what he was thinking — where it might go. But the words had stuck in her throat, and now she might not get another chance.

Twenty-One

ONE OF THE things that'd stuck in Penny's mind since the first day she'd suspected that Buck was her father was her uncertainty about Rowan's reaction. Buck was his stepfather, but there was a connection between the two of them, even if Rowan had hated the man for most of his life. They'd finally had the chance to reconnect, to build a relationship, and Penny's news might derail all of that.

She'd put off telling him over the phone. The right thing would've been to break the news to him as soon as she found out that Buck was her father, not to mention the suspicion she'd shared with the police over Betsy's alibi. But now that he was home, she couldn't avoid it — she had to face him and tell him the truth.

He was due at any moment—he'd called her from the ferry. She was nervous about telling him and how he'd react. She picked up the envelope with the DNA results and shoved it into a kitchen drawer beside a pile of neatly folded tea towels. With a sigh, she shoved the drawer shut. Then opened it. She tugged the envelope free and set it on the bench again.

She'd done the test without consulting him. Would he be upset?

Rob wandered into the kitchen, hair mussed and wearing only a pair of shorts. He had a few days off from work and had come home to the island. All he'd done since he accompanied her to the police station was eat and sleep. She'd barely seen him.

"What's that?" he asked, pulling a cereal box out of the cupboard and setting a bowl on the bench.

Penny chewed the end of a fingernail. "DNA results for my paternity test."

He turned and leaned back against the bench, folding his arms over his chest. "What are you up to, Penelope?"

She huffed. "Ever since I found out that Buck's my father, I've been panicked that maybe Rowan might not want to marry me."

He didn't respond. She couldn't stand the silence.

"Why would he back out of marrying you?"

"I don't know. You tell me! You're the one who never wanted us to get together."

He sighed, looking away. "When we were kids, I heard Mum on the phone talking to June Clements. She inferred that Buck was your father. I've wondered about it ever since. I didn't know that Buck wasn't his biological father at first—we didn't talk about stuff like that as boys. So, when you started dating Rowan... Well, that's why I was so angry about it. It's why I had the rule about dating my friends. No one told me he wasn't Buck's son, and I was suspicious that maybe the two of you were related."

Suddenly it all fell into place. Her brother had been so protective of her, keeping her away from his friends, telling her she couldn't date them. But what he'd meant was she couldn't date Rowan. She raised a hand to cover her mouth. "You knew Buck was my father?"

"I suspected. I didn't know. And I've never said anything to Rowan about it."

"I can't believe this."

"Penny, you've got to let it go. You and Rowan are in love —none of that matters now. Buck is his stepdad—he's not related to you. And Rowan won't be upset to learn about the connection. Well, he might be, but not at you. None of this is your fault. It won't stop him from marrying you. He's a good man."

She was blowing this whole thing out of proportion. "You think I'm being overly dramatic."

He poured cereal into his bowl. "No more than usual."

She slapped his arm playfully. "This is serious, Rob."

"You're getting worked up over nothing. I know this whole situation with Buck has shaken you, but don't take that out on Rowan or your relationship. You've got a good thing going with him, Pen. Don't mess it up. Okay?"

He knew her so well. Too well. Maybe he was right — she could unintentionally sabotage her relationship with Rowan because of how unsettled she felt. Everything in her world had been turned upside down. The things she'd believed about herself were no longer true, the things she'd always wondered over had been confirmed and not in a good way.

It turned out her father knew she existed, but had never wanted to get to know her. Not only that, but he might be a murderer and had definitely taken her mother's innocence. Her family could've featured on a daytime talk show. The drama was getting out of control.

There was a knock at the front door. Rob poured milk over his cereal. "I'm going to give you some space. Good luck, Pen." He kissed her forehead as he walked past with his bowl and headed for his bedroom.

She drew a quick breath, then hurried to the door to answer it. Rowan wore a pair of dark jeans and a casual blue T-shirt that accentuated his lithe physique. He held out a flower to her, then leaned in close to kiss her on the lips. His kiss stole her breath away.

"Welcome home," she whispered as his arms wrapped around her and pulled her to him.

"It's good to be back. I don't think I can stay away so long next time."

* * *

"Buck did what?" Rowan launched from the couch to his feet, eyes blazing.

Penny straightened solemnly. "I know I should've said something, but I thought you might react badly. Surely you can understand that."

"He slept with your mother when she was a teenager? I'm going over there right now to punch him in his smug nose."

He was fuming. Maybe she shouldn't have said anything. But she didn't regret doing the DNA test. She had to know. How could they get married without total honesty? Would he still want to marry her? Questions whirled around in her head, making her dizzy.

"Don't go over there. I don't need you to get arrested for assault. It's in the past — it was a long time ago."

"No, this is ridiculous, Penny. He's a felon in my mind, even if he didn't commit that murder. All this time, I thought he was hiding away because of the rumours around your grandmother's death, but it turns out he was just a pervert after all."

"Um, well, there's been a bit of progress on that front as well. It turns out, he might also be the murderer. We're not sure, but you should prepare yourself."

His eyes widened in shock. "What? Tell me everything." He sat opposite her and leaned forwards to take her hands in his. She shared about her discussion with Betsy and her suspicions over what she'd said. He nodded along, but didn't seem convinced. Then she told him what Bea had found and how the two of them had gone to the police. His face reddened more with every passing moment.

"We're engaged," he said softly. "That means we planned on spending the rest of our lives together. Yet you didn't think to include me in any of this?"

"Planned? As in — past tense?" Her voice wobbled.

He stood and pressed both hands to his hips. "Plan... Planned... What does it matter? I can't believe all this was going on and you didn't say a single word to me. Every phone call with you was lighthearted discussions about possums and injured sea eagles and who was kissing who at the local bush dance. Why didn't you say anything?"

"I'm sorry." He was right — they were getting married. She shouldn't have hidden this from him for so long. If he'd done the same, she'd have been livid with him.

He sat again, poised on the edge of the chair. "Forget it. We'll get better at communicating. Right? We've got forever to learn."

"Right, I'll be better. I promise. I'm still figuring this whole thing out."

"We're moving too fast," he said, reaching for her hand and squeezing it. "I moved too quickly for you."

"No, that's not true. I want this — I promise you, I do. It's going to be okay. But firstly, how do you feel about Buck being my father?"

He leaned back in his chair and looked away. "I don't care..."

"But I do," she said firmly. "And I don't think that's true. You must have feelings about it."

His nostrils flared, but he stayed silent.

"We both have to communicate," she said.

Rowan threw up his hands. "I don't know. If you want me to be honest, I don't know how I feel about it. I'm confused, I'm angry, I'm disgusted."

"Disgusted at me?"

"No!" he shouted. Then he lowered his voice. "No, I'm disgusted with him. As much as he drove me crazy, he's the only father I've ever known. Now to find out..." His voice broke.

Penny stood to her feet and took a step towards him. "You're right — I wish I could make it better. But I can't. I'm still trying to process it all myself. I've been so shaken up by this whole thing — all the lies, the hidden truths, the betrayals. I don't know what or who to believe anymore. I have no idea how to feel. I suppose I didn't tell you because I didn't want to say the words out loud and hear that pain in your voice."

"Everything I believed about my family is a lie." Rowan's voice was soft, his shoulders slumped.

She reached out to him, but he stood, hands raised. It was like a stab to her heart. She slipped the engagement ring he'd given her off her finger and handed it to him.

"Do you want to take this back? I won't blame you."

He took it, his jaw clenched tight. "Why would I want to do that?"

"It looks like Buck killed my grandmother," she said. "We're connected, you and me. But now that connection is tainted by my father, your stepdad, and what he's done."

He blanched. "Are you sure he killed her?"

"Not entirely. I don't want it to be true. We haven't heard anything from the police since I visited the station with Bea, but they may reopen the case and name him a suspect again."

"So, he no longer has an alibi?"

"It's possible."

He reached out for her and pulled her into an embrace, cupping her head with one hand against his chest. "I'm sorry,

Pen. That's a lot for you to deal with on your own. I wish I'd been here with you."

"It's fine," she said numbly. "I'll understand if you need time. This whole thing is getting messy. It could tear both our families apart."

He slid the ring back onto her finger carefully, then kissed it. "Whatever happens, we'll face it together."

"Together." Her heart thudded against her ribcage as he pulled her close.

"And no more secrets," he added.

"Total honesty," she agreed.

Later, as he walked out the front door, Penny felt as though her heart might break into small pieces. She didn't want him to go. It was a new feeling, this intense desire to spend every moment together. When they were married, they wouldn't have to say goodbye any longer. She couldn't wait for that day. But for now, she would have to spend the rest of the night running over the events of the past in her mind, wondering how things might've gone differently. How much pain her mother had endured alone during her younger years. How she'd missed out on a lifetime of love with the grandmother her mother had always described in only the warmest tones.

She leaned her back against the door, then slid to the floor, tucking her knees to her chest. Memories flooded her thoughts —of her mother, her childhood, the ghost of a grandmother she couldn't recall but who'd always had a presence through her absence. The father she'd never known but had pictured in her mind since the earliest of years. She tugged her mobile phone from her pocket and dialled.

"Hi, Mum. Let's talk..."

Twenty–Two

IT WAS SATURDAY, and Bea had taken the day off to spend it with Harry. He'd been resting at her father's house most of the week and seemed to be in good spirits when she came home on Friday night. She'd suggested they sit on the dunes and paint beachscapes the following day, and he'd agreed. She dragged a folding table out to the edge of the dunes, along with two folding chairs. Then she set up canvases and paints before Harry came and joined her.

He was gaunt and pale. She wore a wide-brimmed straw hat and a light summer dress. They both donned aprons from the kitchen drawer.

"I have no idea what to paint," Harry said. "I'm not very good at this. I don't think I've painted anything since seventh grade."

Bea mixed red and blue together on her palette. "Paint anything you like — you can do the entire landscape, or you can pick one element and focus on that. I'm going to paint that tree with the bird sitting on the lowest branch. See it?"

He glanced up. "Do you mean the rosella?"

"That's the one."

"I might paint the whole beach."

"Good idea. It's such a pretty scene."

They got to work. Bea took her time mixing the exact colours she needed for the purple flowers on the bush, the smoky green for the leaves of the tree, and the bright reds and blues for the rosella's feathers. Harry used a charcoal pencil to sketch the scene of the beach, the water and the distant rocky outcropping over his canvas.

"How are you feeling today, honey?"

He shrugged. "I've had some heart palpitations, and I think I've got a bit of a fever. I'm tired all the time, but not so bad as I was."

"We'll have to talk to the doctor about those palpitations," Bea said, her words tinged with worry.

"I'll give him a call after this. Staying here on the island and relaxing is helping, I think. That, plus the antibiotics. Before I knew what was wrong with me, I was pushing myself too hard. At uni, I kept attending classes, doing assignments, studying for exams. I was working at that corner store every spare moment I had. Looking back, I should've taken some downtime to recover."

"Hindsight is twenty-twenty. At least you're getting the medicine and rest you need now. We can only hope you'll be well in time for next semester."

"I can't believe I'm saying this, but I miss uni."

"I'm glad to hear it." Bea dipped her brush in paint. "If you didn't miss it, I'd be worried. University is one of the best times of life — so much fun, you get to choose what you study, see your friends every day, learn how to be independent and make your own choices. I'm glad you're enjoying it."

"It's good. But it's hard, too. Not the study—I'm enjoying that—but the people."

"Oh?" He didn't often open up. Bea had wondered how he was coping with living out of home and making new friends. But whenever she asked, he'd give a noncommittal answer or grunt in response.

"I was seeing this girl for a while. I really liked her, but she broke up with me before the end of the semester."

"I'm sorry, honey."

"It's fine. But I kind of ditched my friends to spend time with her over the past few months. So, now that we're broken up, I don't have anyone."

She covered the canvas with long, steady strokes of paint as she considered her words. "Perhaps you could apologise?"

"I don't know," he replied. "We were new friends. Most of the kids I went to school with ended up at different universities, and none of them are in my degree program. So, I'd only recently met them all. Now they've moved on and don't seem to want me around."

"What happened with your girlfriend?" She tried not to sound too interested, but it was his first girlfriend and she hadn't even known the woman existed. She wanted to know every detail, but if she pushed too hard, he'd retreat.

"Jocelyn? She said she has to focus on studying and doesn't have time for a relationship. We're in all the same classes together. So, it's been hard. I feel completely alone."

His words broke Bea's heart. She hated to see him face any kind of difficulty. In her mind, he was still the little boy with the unruly brown curls whose chubby cheeks she could kiss to make everything better. "I'm sorry. I know that must've been difficult to hear. But it sounds like you're in different places."

"I guess so." He frowned as he filled in the sand on his painting with a golden yellow he'd mixed together. "Love is hard."

"That's very true."

"How did you manage it when Dad left you? What did you do to move on?"

She sighed. "It's not easy after so many years. But I had to build new relationships, change my thought patterns…"

"Change your thought patterns?" His eyebrows knotted together.

"Yes. If I was thinking about your father, letting myself be hateful or angry, I chose instead to replace those thoughts with something else — maybe something positive about him, or about a topic I'm interested in, or a hobby I enjoy, or a friendship I like… I tried not to dwell too much on the bad stuff. I didn't always succeed. There were plenty of times when I was very angry. But I kept trying, and I got better and better over time at changing my thought patterns."

"That makes sense, I guess. But it's harder than it sounds."

"It's definitely not easy. If I'd let myself wallow, though, I'd still be angry and resentful. Instead, I've forgiven him, I'm positive about the future, I wish nothing but good things for your dad, and I'm happy I get to be here on Coral Island with you. There's a lot in my life to be grateful for."

She reached out a hand to pat his arm.

"Dad seems happy too," he said.

She inhaled a sharp breath, then reminded herself how happy and grateful she was. Again. "I'm glad to hear it."

"I spoke to him on the phone last night. He said he's going to ask Annie to marry him."

Bea's lips pulled into a thin line. "Engaged again? Wow, he sure does like to get engaged."

"You're not upset about it, are you, Mum?"

She forced a smile. "Not really. Well, maybe a little bit. It does seem strange the way he keeps on proposing."

"He doesn't like being alone. And I think this one will stick. He says they're in love."

"That's great." She did her best to keep the sarcasm from her voice. Every time she felt as though she'd managed to put her feelings of resentment behind her, something happened to

164

change it. Most of the time, it was her ex-husband getting engaged to a new woman. How many more times would it happen before she could be blasé about it? The thought made her giggle.

"What's funny?" Harry asked.

"Oh, nothing. Just imagining your dad... Well, never mind. I'd better not say. I'm still working on being happy for him, so you may have to give me a few minutes."

Harry laughed along with her. "You're hilarious, Mum."

"I try."

* * *

Three weeks later, the weather had turned warmer still. Bea stood at the café door and looked across the bay. The mainland was hidden beneath a thicket of dark, swirling clouds. Thunder boomed in the distance. A storm was on its way to the island.

Aidan's truck pulled up outside the café. Harry climbed out of the passenger side. His cheeks had a little more colour, and he'd been spending more time outdoors in the past week. He seemed to be on the mend, and Bea was grateful. There was nothing more gratifying to her than witnessing her child coming back to life after he'd spent so many weeks barely leaving his bed.

"We came to get a milkshake from the best café in town," Aidan said.

The two of them had hit it off in recent weeks. They'd bonded over football. Aidan had sat and watched game after game with Harry while he was recuperating, and she'd never seen her son show so much interest in the national sport as he had while Aidan cheered, shouted and stomped around the living room beside him, depending on how well his team was doing. After the football games, they'd gone fishing, then as

Harry's health improved, Aidan had taken him out on the boat to snorkel off Point Prospect. Bea was delighted to see the two of them forming a fast friendship.

"Come inside. I'll take care of you," she said.

Just as they were about to step into the café, Taya shouted at them all from across the street, one arm waving wildly over her head. Penny stood beside her, and the two of them hurried over to greet Bea, Aidan and Harry. Taya and Penny kissed her cheek, then Aidan's cheek, and fussed over Harry.

"You're looking so much better," Penny said, tipping her head to one side to smile up at Harry. He loomed over her petite frame, but his cheeks were pink at her words.

"Thanks, I feel pretty good. At least compared to before."

"That's good to hear," Taya replied.

Evie poked her head through the door of her bookshop. "What's going on out here? Move along, please. You're causing a commotion."

They all chortled over her fierce expression, then with a laugh, she joined them, still wearing her retail apron.

"We're getting a milkshake," Aidan explained. "You should join us."

"I'd love that. I'm exhausted, my feet ache and my head is pounding. We had so many tourists through the shop today, I didn't get a chance to eat any lunch. But it's quiet now. I'm about to put up the closed sign. Then I'll come over to the café and we can celebrate."

"What are we celebrating?" Bea asked.

"Harry's health, Penny's engagement, Taya's new job. Pick one, or maybe we'll celebrate them all."

"I like your way of thinking," Taya said.

"This calls for chocolate," Bea added. "I've got a deliciously decadent mud cake with our names on it."

A man walked up the steps to the bookshop's front door, his head down, a cap pulled low over his forehead.

"Sorry!" Evie called. "We're closed."

He glanced up, and Bea recognised him immediately. It was Buck Clements. She'd never seen him at the bookshop or the café before. In fact, she couldn't recall spotting him around Kellyville. He seemed to mostly stay within the confines of Amity Point as far as she was aware. Yet there he was, right on Evie's front steps, only metres away from where all of them stood gaping.

"Sorry, I was hoping to get Penny's number from you. But I can see she's right here in front of me, so there's no need. Hello, Penny. Do you think I could get a word in private? I went to the wildlife refuge, but no one answered the buzzer."

"That's because I'm here," Penny said, her voice trembling.

"I can see that."

"Penny, do you want me to come with you?" Bea asked.

Penny shook her head. "I'll be fine. I'll join you in a minute. Okay?"

Bea didn't want to leave her. It was possible Buck had found out about Penny's testimony against him and had come to seek revenge.

"We can't go inside without her," she whispered.

Aidan stepped forwards. "We'll be right here."

Penny walked gingerly towards her father. They spoke together quietly for a few moments before Penny's voice raised in protest.

"You can't say that! It's not fair. You were the one at fault. You were an adult. What you did was wrong."

"We were in love," he said, his voice laced with anger. "You don't understand."

"That wasn't love," Penny said.

"Is everything okay?" Bea asked, hurrying to her friend's side and sliding her hand into Penny's, which was shaking.

"Buck was just leaving."

He shook his head, eyes red-rimmed. "I made mistakes. I know that. But I've paid a penance for decades because of it. Why do you think I kept away? I was ashamed."

"You killed my grandmother, you took advantage of my mother... What else is there to say?" Penny's cheeks were wet with tears.

Buck's eyes widened. "What? No..."

A police cruiser pulled up behind them in the street. The strobe lights on top of the vehicle began to flash, and the siren blared a single loud sound that momentarily deafened Bea. She used her free hand to cover one ear.

"What on earth?"

The police officer she'd given the box of evidence to stepped out of the vehicle. His face was grim, and he walked towards them.

"Buck Clements?"

Buck glanced at the officer, his face growing pale. "Yes?"

"You're under arrest for the murder of Mary Brown..."

As the officer placed Buck under arrest, Bea pulled Penny back and out of the way. Her friend seemed immobile, as though she couldn't process what was happening. Her tears had stopped, and her hand no longer shook, but was cold to the touch.

"Come on, Pen. Let's go inside," she said.

"I want to see..."

"Sir." Aidan stepped forwards. "Officer, can you tell us what's going on?"

"The investigation into Mary Brown's murder was reopened several weeks ago, after further evidence came to light in the case. I can't go into details, as it could impact the integrity of the charges. But this man is currently under arrest for that murder. If you come down to the station, we can talk about what comes next."

"Thank you," Aidan said, exchanging a meaningful look with Bea.

The box she found must've given them the evidence they needed to arrest Buck. That along with Penny's questioning of his alibi. Maybe they'd spoken to Betsy and discovered that she had lied to cover for her brother after all. She wished she could ask the officer a dozen questions to find out more.

If they were arresting him, they must have everything they needed to make the charges stick, as they'd been reluctant to charge him previously. Bea and Penny had helped them solve the case. Her head spun with a feeling of euphoria.

As the police vehicle drove away with Buck handcuffed in the back seat, Bea watched it with one hand cupped over her eyes. Her gaze drifted from the vehicle as it turned the corner and landed on Betsy's frail form. She stood in front of her flower shop, one hand held to her heart, her eyes on the retreating form of her brother hunched in the back of the car. Bea felt sorry for her, but she couldn't muster up any sympathy for Buck. He should've been in those cuffs decades ago. Finally, justice for Penny's family would be served.

She squeezed Penny's hand. Her friend seemed to come to life with a jolt.

"Well, that was exciting."

"Are you okay? I know you wanted to get to know him, since he's your father..."

"I was willing to give him the benefit of the doubt at first. But as soon as I suspected Betsy had lied for him when she gave the police her alibi, I couldn't stop thinking about it. He's a murderer. He killed my grandmother, he destroyed my mother's life, he left me with a broken family. He deserves everything he gets."

Twenty-Three

THE WATER WAS warm against her skin. Penny lay on her back on the board, letting the sway of the swell beneath her rock her into a state of near sleep. The sun overhead glared in her eyes, so she shut them and rested a forearm over her face. There was no better place to be than out on the water. There was no surf to mention, so instead she languished on her board, enjoying the salty flavour of her lips, the heat of the sun on her wetsuit, the gentle sound of water lapping against the edge of the board and bubbling to shore.

With a sigh, she rolled over and sat up, straddling the board. The ocean was clear with a hint of bright blue. She could see the sand several metres down, as though looking through thick glass. A small school of brightly coloured fish darted beneath her board. The shadow of a bank of clouds drifted across her body and out to sea.

She couldn't imagine living anywhere other than Coral Island. It held her heart. She'd moved away briefly when she was younger to study marine biology at university. But she'd returned as soon as she was able, when a long-term boyfriend had broken her heart and an internship at a marine outpost had ended. After that, she used the island as a base — leaving to undertake projects with various marine research teams around the world. But finally she'd developed the idea of opening the wildlife refuge and saved the money to add to a government grant she won to build it.

It'd been a dream of hers, and it'd come true. She'd had no idea how hard it would be to make that dream a reality or to keep it running. The pressure she was under every single month to pay the bills that continued piling up had given her a stomach ulcer five years earlier. She'd made it through that particular period with a more mature outlook. She was wiser now, or so she'd thought. But then she'd let herself slack on the administrative tasks — they weren't her strong suit. She'd much rather be out bandaging broken limbs or spoon-feeding baby animals than filing paperwork. She'd staved off bankruptcy with a new grant, but how long would she be able to keep going this way?

And now she was engaged to be married. Had she thought it through? Where would they live? What would they do? She couldn't leave the refuge. Surely Rowan knew that. But if they remained on the island, what would he do for a living? He was an international journalist. He'd have to continue traveling, and what would that look like for them? Could they maintain a relationship that way?

His truck pulled up outside her beach house, and she tented a hand over her eyes, squinting into the glare to see him climb out and walk to the front door. He soon reappeared, then waved in her direction. She waved back, paddled to shore.

"No surf today?" he asked when she padded dripping up the sand, the board beneath her arm.

"Nothing. Not even a whisper of a breeze." She reached up to plant a salty kiss on his soft lips.

"Storm brewing?"

"Maybe tomorrow," she suggested.

"Can we talk?"

"I'll get dressed and meet you on the back porch."

She showered and dressed quickly, still towelling her hair dry as she walked through the house and into the kitchen. She grabbed a round tray and piled glasses, a pitcher of orange juice, crackers, cheese, olives and a cheese knife onto the tray and carried it all out to the back porch where Rowan sat, arms resting on his thighs as he stared out to sea.

"You look beautiful today."

"Thank you," she said. "It's my beach look."

"It suits you."

She handed him a glass of juice, then sat beside him, one hand on his thigh. All of her concerns and questions about their relationship — the hasty engagement, the future — faded into nothing with him seated here beside her. She wanted to spend her life with him. Couldn't imagine living any other way. It was like a hunger deep inside her gut that couldn't be satisfied without Rowan in her life.

"I had to come and see you," he said. "We haven't really talked about what happened yesterday."

"You mean the arrest?"

"You left a message on my voicemail."

"I didn't want you to find out from someone else."

"Thanks," he replied as he took her hand and wove his fingers through hers. "It was a bit of a shock. I went over to Mum's to see how she's doing. She was smoking again."

"I thought she quit."

"Ten years ago."

"Did she say anything?" Penny asked.

"Just that she was glad it was over." Rowan exhaled slowly. "I think she always suspected he'd killed your grandmother. She didn't say so, but I'm fairly sure it's why she left him in the end. After Bea's mother took her life, Mum changed. She blamed him, I think. And they fought constantly — at the time, I didn't understand what they were fighting about but now, looking back, that was it. I'm pretty sure. I asked her about it, but she wouldn't answer me. She just stared into the distance, smoking."

"Wow, that's really incredible. All this time, she knew..."

"Maybe Bea's mother knew as well." Rowan shrugged. "I suppose we'll never fully understand what happened."

"Change of subject?" Penny asked, turning to face Rowan and crisscrossing her legs.

"What's up?"

"What happens after we get married?"

He grinned, leaned in close and kissed her cheek, then her nose, then her lips. "Oh, we're having *the* talk?"

Her cheeks flushed. "No, not that kind of talk. I meant, where will we live? What will we do? Do you want kids? What are your dreams?"

He laughed. "Ah, okay, I see — you want to have the other talk. Let's see... I assumed we'd live here, since your refuge is here. You can't really live anywhere else, can you?"

"No, I can't leave the island."

"Then that's settled. And as for what we'll do, I'm not sure. If you want to keep doing what you're doing, that's great. But I'm ready for a change. I'm afraid I'm really not sure what that will mean for me at this stage, though. I'm not qualified for anything other than journalism. Maybe there are some local rags that would give me a chance, but that might not be a full-time gig."

"Do you want to do that? Work casually for local newspapers?"

"Not really. I'm fairly sick of the whole thing, honestly. I'd probably prefer to work on a fishing boat than write a story. I'm burned out, Pen. I'd be happy to do something completely different to what I've been doing. Maybe I'll get a retail job, or I could teach scuba diving down at the marina."

Penny laughed. "Wow. So, a complete and utter turn-around, then?"

"I'm open to anything."

"That's good to hear. Because I don't like the idea of you being gone all the time, chasing stories."

"I've saved a nest egg. I haven't had many expenses over the years, and I invested in real estate early," he said. "So I don't really have to work full-time. But I'd like to do something with my days. I'm not really the type to sit around and stare at my belly button."

She traced a circle on his arm with her fingertip. "It sounds to me like you're in need of a break. We could get married, take an extended honeymoon, and then when we come back, you could be a house husband for a while, just until you figure out what you want to do next."

"I like the sound of that," he replied. "I'll wait on you hand and foot. I'll cook your favourite meals and wash your clothes. Then when you get home at night, I can kiss..."

She pressed a finger to his lips. "Hold that thought. I'm going to put on some music. I'll be right back."

He groaned as she walked away. "You have the worst taste in music. That's something else we need to discuss — I'm going to have to be the DJ in our relationship. No more dance music, I beg of you. Please, rock and roll only."

She laughed as she selected a classic rock album she knew he loved and carried the speaker outside to sit on the table.

"The last thing you wanted to talk about was children, right?" He picked up an olive and popped it into his mouth.

"That's right." Her stomach clenched. She'd been nervous to have this conversation. At forty-six years of age, their only real option was adoption. If he was set on having children naturally, he was likely to be disappointed.

"I'm not sure how you feel about kids, but I've never really wanted any of my own. My childhood was so full of conflict and upheaval, I didn't want to put any kid through that. Of course, I know we'd be better parents than mine were." He rolled his eyes. "Clearly, even a crazy cat would be a better father than the one who raised me. But it's hard for me to get my head around the idea of bringing children into this world, especially after all I've seen on the job."

She released a sigh of relief. "I'm glad to hear you say that. There was a time when I'd hoped I would be able to settle down and have children with someone. But then the years rolled by, and I realised I was happy on my own without them. Now, of course, it's too late for anything other than adoption. But I don't think I want that either. I have my animals, and I'm happy with them and with you."

"We're on the same page, then?"

"I think so." She laughed. "That was easier than I'd thought it would be."

"I love you, Penelope St James," he said, pulling her into his lap and enveloping her with his strong arms.

She nestled into his chest. "I love you right back, Rowan Clements."

"Oh, about that," he said. "I'm changing my last name to Hathaway, my mother's maiden name. I don't want anything more to do with Buck or his name. I hope you don't mind."

She arched an eyebrow. "So, I'll be Penelope Hathaway?"

"If you want to be."

Her hands snuck around his neck. "I can't wait."

* * *

The flight from Sydney back to Prosperine was a short one. Bea yawned when the plane taxied down the runway and stopped on the hot tarmac. She'd accompanied Harry back to Sydney. He couldn't study again until the following semester, but he'd wanted to go back to his flat and get back to his life.

He'd work at the local corner store for the rest of the semester, then travel to Coral Island for the summer holidays and return to Sydney when the new year began.

In the meantime, he could catch up with some study, spend time with friends and save a little money. He'd begun to get itchy feet living so long on the island, and the medicine and rest had done wonders for his health. He still had a few aches and pains, and a little fatigue if he overdid things, but was otherwise in much better health.

She walked across the tarmac to the shuttle bus and climbed aboard. How many times would she do this trip in the years to come? With both her children still living in Sydney, she imagined it would be a regular occurrence.

Harry had lived with her in the cottage now for several months, and she'd loved every moment of it. He was such a funny, sweet, caring boy. She'd miss his jokes and the way he made her a drink when she got home from work and sat with her on the verandah to listen to her tales about the tourists who'd come into the café throughout the day. She'd miss game nights on Friday and movie nights with popcorn laced with her famous salted caramel sauce that he loved so much.

It might've been illness that caused him to stay so long, but she'd enjoyed the chance to relive his youth again, at least for a little while. She missed having her children at home with her every day. When they were young, she thought they'd never be independent or that she could have time to herself, but it'd come faster than she'd believed possible, and now she was an empty nester with a cottage all to herself.

The shuttle bus dropped her at the ferry station. As she eyed the ferry terminal, she wished she was already home. She was exhausted. It'd been a long day — they'd begun early with breakfast at Harry's favourite restaurant near his flat. Then she'd spent the rest of the day traveling. Now, with the sun setting behind her, she still had a ferry ride to the island and then had to drive home and find something to eat for dinner. Her feet ached, her head pounded and she'd run out of water in her bottle an hour earlier. Her throat was parched.

"Beatrice Rushton. What a surprise," a deep voice said.

She spun around to see Aidan behind her, a wide grin on his tanned face.

She squealed and ran to him, throwing her arms around his neck and planting a kiss on his lips. "I can't believe you came to meet me. You have no idea how glad I am to see you."

He laughed. "I thought it might be a nice surprise."

"I can hardly put one foot in front of the other, I'm starving and I missed you — so you thought right. Thank you!"

"I've also made a dinner reservation at a delicious Italian restaurant on the main drag in Airlie Beach," he said.

She frowned. "Really? But isn't this the last ferry?"

"I brought my boat over. You can travel back to the island in style."

She kissed him again. "That is the best news I've had all day."

He held out an arm for her to take. "Ready to eat?"

"Let's go. Italian food is my absolute favourite."

"This place is great," he said. "They have a veal ravioli that will rock your world."

* * *

Aidan was right about the ravioli. Beatrice pushed a piece of the pasta into her mouth, her eyes drifting shut, and chewed in delight. She swallowed and reached for her glass of red wine.

"That's the best ravioli I've ever eaten."

"I thought you'd like it," he replied, spinning his fork around in the spaghetti.

"The sauce is light, the veal is cooked to perfection, and the herbs are divine."

"It's one of my favourites," he said. "But still not as good as your lasagne."

She grinned. "You have to say that."

"No, it's true. Nothing comes close to that."

"Aww... You're the best. I think I'll keep you."

"Is that a promise?" he asked, one eyebrow raised.

"If you'd like it to be." Her heart was full, and her stomach soon followed. Beatrice didn't know what the future held for her and Aidan, but she knew she wanted them to be together. They would both live on Coral Island. She in her beach cottage, him in his immaculate and stylish house. They'd run their businesses and eat delicious food and spend every spare moment they could manage together.

After so many years married to a man who didn't appreciate her and twisting her life around so that it would fit his, it was a respite and a relief to have such freedom. They loved each other, they were there for each other, they each had their own lives and made their own choices. That was enough for her, for now. It was everything she needed.

Twenty-Four

BETSY'S CAR pulled up in front of Frank's house. Beside her in the passenger seat, Samantha chattered on about school, how she'd won the spelling bee and how her best friend had told her she didn't want to be friends anymore.

"But I told her I don't want to be her friend then, either," Sam continued. "So she said she's not going to invite me to her birthday party. And I said, fine, I don't want to go anyway. But I couldn't say I wouldn't invite her to my party because I don't ever have one. Dad doesn't like to throw parties. Says they're far too much work. But it doesn't matter because then she said she was sorry and she would always be my friend, and of course I was invited to her party, and we made up."

Sam glanced up at Betsy as she pulled on the handbrake as though waiting for affirmation.

"Sounds like you handled that just right," Betsy said, patting her granddaughter on the hand affectionately. "Now, let's go inside and see if Dad's home yet."

"There's his car in the garage," Sam said.

The garage door was open, and the car sat inside. Betsy noticed it had a ding in the bumper and seemed lopsided as though one of the tyres was flat. She'd have to ask Frank if he needed some financial help to get it fixed. Of course, he wouldn't like that. He was fiercely independent. Always had been, ever since he got engaged to Sam's mother and pushed Betsy out of his life.

Sam bounded out of the car, her school backpack slung over one shoulder. She ducked through the garage and into the house via the side door. Betsy followed slowly, cautious over how Frank would react to her coming inside.

Usually, she dropped Sam off outside and waited until she'd gone inside before pulling out of the driveway and heading home. But today, she wanted to talk to Frank about what'd happened with Buck. It was time he knew about his uncle's arrest. She doubted he would've heard via the grapevine. Frank rarely spoke to anyone on the island and kept mostly to himself.

She found him in the kitchen heating up a frozen pie for dinner.

"You want a pie?" he asked Sam as she threw her lunch box on the sink.

"Yes, please," she replied before racing off to her room, backpack bouncing against her leg.

"Hi, Frank," Betsy said softly.

He spun to face her. "Oh, hi. I didn't realise you were still here."

"Sorry, I followed Sam in because I wanted to talk to you about something. I hope that's okay."

"Too late now if it's not," he mumbled, setting the pies inside the oven and flicking it on.

"I won't take long. It's about your uncle. He's been arrested."

Frank straightened and crossed his arms. "Oh? What for?"

"Mary Brown's murder."

One eyebrow arched. "Is that so? About time, isn't it?"

She swallowed hard. Did he always have to be so ungrateful? It was difficult for her to face the reality that her son truly seemed to hate her. "I hoped you might have a little more grace for him than that. After all, he's family."

"He's your family, not mine."

"He's your uncle, and that's family," she snapped. Then she smoothed her voice over again. She didn't want to anger him. This was how it always went with them. She'd start out with good intentions, but they'd end up yelling at one another, he'd misunderstand something she said, and the next thing she knew, he'd cast her out of his and Sam's lives.

Frank sighed and studied her, his head wagging slowly back and forth. "We haven't been a family in a long time. I don't owe that man any loyalty. And he deserves to be in jail. Should've been there long ago. Your alibi kept him out and you know it."

"I spoke up because I knew he didn't do it." She pushed a strand of grey curls out of her eyes with a jab.

"He's guilty," Frank spat.

"He's not," she responded. "And you'd know that if you gave him the time of day. We're family, and family sticks together. I lied for him just like I lied for you. Every time you've ever needed me to protect you, I have. Because that's what family does. We protect each other." She stepped forward, raising her hands towards him the way she used to when he was a child, inviting him to embrace her.

But he retreated. "I never asked you to lie for me. And as for him being family... I have no idea whether or not that's true." His arms unfolded, and he pulled out one of the kitchen drawers. When he drew a piece of paper from the drawer, her brow furrowed. What was he talking about? What was he doing?

"I found this," he said. "I did some research and found it down at the library. It's a photocopy of an article from 1972 about someone called Betsy Alton from California. Do you know that name?"

Betsy's stomach flipped. All the blood rushed from her face. "What are you doing?"

"She looks remarkably like you do in all those old photos, but you said you were from Indiana. Right? You want to talk about family? I'm talking about family. And it's time you gave me some answers."

"I'll answer your questions, but you've got to give me a chance," she sobbed.

"The first question I have is — what's your real name, Mother?"

* * *

Continue the series...

Ready to read book 4 in the *Coral Island* series so you can keep following Beatrice, Aidan and the rest of the Coral Island crew? Buy the next book in this series!

Want to find out about all of my new releases? You can get on my VIP reader list by subscribing via my website, and you'll also get a free book.

Also by Lilly Mirren

WOMEN'S FICTION

CORAL ISLAND SERIES

The Island

After twenty five years of marriage and decades caring for her two children, on the evening of their vow renewal, her husband shocks her with the news that he's leaving her.

The Beach Cottage

Beatrice is speechless. It's something she never expected — a secret daughter. She and Aidan have only just renewed their romance, after decades apart, and he never mentioned a child. Did he know she existed?

The Blue Shoal Inn

Taya's inn is in trouble. Her father has built a fancy new resort in Blue Shoal and hired a handsome stranger to manage it. When the stranger offers to buy her inn and merge it with the resort, she wants to hate him but when he rescues a stray dog her feelings for him change.

Island Weddings

Charmaine moves to Coral Island and lands a job working at a local florist shop. It seems as though the entire island has caught wedding fever, with weddings planned every weekend. It's a good opportunity for her to get to know the locals, but what she doesn't expect is to be thrown into the middle of a family drama.

The Island Bookshop

Evie's book club friends are the people in the world she relies on most. But when one of the newer members finds herself confronted with her past, the rest of the club will do what they can to help, endangering the existence of the bookshop without realising it.

An Island Reunion

It's been thirty five years since the friends graduated from Coral Island State Primary School and the class is returning to the island to celebrate.

THE WARATAH INN SERIES

The Waratah Inn

Wrested back to Cabarita Beach by her grandmother's sudden death, Kate Summer discovers a mystery buried in the past that changes everything.

One Summer in Italy

Reeda leaves the Waratah Inn and returns to Sydney, her husband, and her thriving interior design business, only to find her marriage in tatters. She's lost sight of what she wants in life and can't recognise the person she's become.

The Summer Sisters

Set against the golden sands and crystal clear waters of Cabarita Beach three sisters inherit an inn and discover a mystery about their grandmother's past that changes everything they thought they knew about their family...

Christmas at The Waratah Inn

Liz Cranwell is divorced and alone at Christmas. When her friends convince her to holiday at The Waratah Inn, she's dreading her first Christmas on her own. Instead she discovers that strangers can be the balm to heal the wounds of a lonely heart in this heartwarming Christmas story.

EMERALD COVE SERIES

Cottage on Oceanview Lane

When a renowned book editor returns to her roots, she rediscovers her strength & her passion in this heartwarming novel.

Seaside Manor Bed & Breakfast

The Seaside Manor Bed and Breakfast has been an institution in Emerald Cove for as long as anyone can remember. But things are changing and Diana is nervous about what the future might hold for her and her husband, not to mention the historic business.

Bungalow on Pelican Way

Moving to the Cove gave Rebecca De Vries a place to hide from her abusive ex. Now that he's in jail, she can get back to living her life as a police officer in her adopted hometown working alongside her intractable but very attractive boss, Franklin.

Chalet on Cliffside Drive

At forty-four years of age, Ben Silver thought he'd never find love. When he moves to Emerald Cove, he does it to support his birth mother, Diana, after her husband's sudden death. But then he meets Vicky.

Christmas in Emerald Cove

The Flannigan family has been through a lot together. They've grown and changed over the years and now have a blended and extended family that doesn't always see eye to eye. But this Christmas they'll learn that love can overcome all of the pain and differences of the past in this inspiring Christmas tale.

HOME SWEET HOME SERIES

Home Sweet Home

Trina is starting over after a painful separation from her husband of almost twenty years. Grief and loss force her to return to her hometown where she has to deal with all of the things she left behind to rebuild her life, piece by piece; a hometown she hasn't visited since high school graduation.

No Place Like Home

Lisa never thought she'd leave her high-profile finance job in the city to work in a small-town bakery. She also never expected to still be single in her forties.

HISTORICAL FICTION

Beyond the Crushing Waves

An emotional standalone historical saga. Two children plucked from poverty & forcibly deported from the UK to Australia. Inspired by true events. An unforgettable tale of loss, love, redemption & new beginnings.

Under a Sunburnt Sky

Inspired by a true story. Jan Kostanski is a normal Catholic boy in Warsaw when the nazis invade. He's separated from his neighbours, a Jewish family who he considers kin, by the ghetto wall. Jan and his mother decide that they will do whatever it takes to save their Jewish friends from certain death. The unforgettable tale of an everyday family's fight against evil, and the unbreakable bonds of their love.

MYSTERIES

White Picket Lies

Fighting the demons of her past Toni finds herself in the midst of a second marriage breakdown at forty seven years of age. She struggles to keep depression at bay while doing her best to raise a wayward teenaged son and uncover the identity of the killer.

In this small town investigation, it's only a matter of time until friends and neighbours turn on each other.

Cast of Characters

As the *Coral Island* series grows, the cast of characters does too. I hope this handy reference will help you keep them sorted!

* * *

Aidan Whitlock - former professional footballer, current primary school PE teacher.

Andrew Reddy - The new manager at *Paradise Resort*.

Annie Draper - Bea's friend from Sydney.

Beatrice Rushton - previously married and living in Sydney, now a resident of Coral Island.

Betsy Norton - Elderly, American, owns the florist shop.

Bradford Rushton - Bea's younger brother, owns a charter fishing company out of Airlie Beach.

Brett O'Hanley - Beatrice & Aidan's contractor.

Buck Clements - Rowan's step father and June's ex-husband.

Camden Futcher - Taya's adult daughter, training to become a chef in Cairns.

Cameron Eldridge - Taya's father and owner of *Paradise Resorts*.

Charmaine Billings - new resident of Coral Island, works at Betsy's Florals.

Danita Pike - Bea's adult daughter, lives in Sydney.

Elias Rushton - Bea's father, lives on Coral Island.

Eveleigh (Evie) Mair - Owner of *Eveleigh's Books*, the book shop attached the *Bea's Coffee*.

Frank Norton - Betsy's adult son and Samantha's father.

Fudge - Beatrice's pug.

Grace Allen - Aidan's teenaged daughter.

Harry Pike - Bea's adult son, lives in Sydney.

June Clements - proprietor of the *Coral Cafe* & Rowan's mother.

Kelly Allen - Grace's mother & Aidan's ex-girlfriend.

Luella Rushton - Bea's mother, deceased.

Mary Brown - Penny's grandmother, murder victim.

Ms Gossamer - librarian in Kellyville.

Penny St James - Owner of the Coral Island Wildlife Rescue centre.

Preston Pike - Bea's ex-husband, lives between Sydney & Melbourne.

Robert St James - Penny's brother, travels around to work in construction.

Rowan Clements - June Clements' son, journalist.

Ruby Brown - Penny's mother.

Samantha Norton - Betsy's granddaughter & Frank's daughter.

Taya Eldridge - Owns the Blue Shoal Inn, is Cameron & Tina Eldridge's daughter.

Tina Eldridge - Taya's mother, married to Cameron.

Todd Futcher - Taya's former husband, deceased.

About the Author

Lilly Mirren is an Amazon top 20, Audible top 15 and USA Today Bestselling author who has sold over one million copies of her books worldwide. She lives in Brisbane, Australia with her husband and three children.

She always dreamed of being a writer and is now living that dream. Her books combine heartwarming storylines with realistic characters readers can't get enough of.

Her debut series, The Waratah Inn, set in the delightful Cabarita Beach, hit the *USA Today* Bestseller list and since then, has touched the hearts of hundreds of thousands of readers across the globe.

Made in the USA
Monee, IL
08 January 2023

24850691R00121